"An exciting story FULL OF HEART."
—Kristine Jelstrom-Hamill, Buttonwood Books and Toys

"A fluid meshing of loyalty, forgiveness, and trust will leave readers hoping that the author has MORE ONE-AND-ONLY STORIES TO TELL."
—*Publishers Weekly* (starred review)

"Ultimately a tale of FRIENDSHIP AND FORGIVENESS."
—*Bulletin of the Center for Children's Books*

"Katherine Applegate has DONE IT AGAIN."
—Marilyn Robbins, BookBar Inc.

"Delightfully heartfelt and ADVENTUROUS."
—*School Library Journal* (starred review)

"SWEET AND REDEMPTIVE."
—Sam Miller, Carmichael's Bookstore

"Explores themes of forgiveness, REDEMPTION, and HEROISM."
—*The Horn Book*

"GOOD DOG, BOB." —Danny DeVito

looking

Ivan used to ask me what I did when I wasn't hanging out at the Exit 8 Big Top Mall and Video Arcade.

I wasn't like the rest of the animals. Caged, trapped.

I told him I was scrounging for food. And he never questioned it.

When you think about it, though, where's a better place to find food than the floor of a mall at the end of the day?

Yeah. I wasn't looking for food.

I was looking for her.

For Boss.

KATHERINE

The

ONE AND

ON

illustrations by
Patricia Castelao

APPLEGATE

LY BOB

HARPER
An Imprint of HarperCollins*Publishers*

ISBN 978-0-06-299132-4

Typography by Sarah Piersen
22 23 24 25 26 LBC 9 8 7 6 5
❖
First trade paperback edition, 2022

for my family:
human, feline,
and—of course—canine

For small creatures such as we
the vastness is bearable only through love.
—Carl Sagan

To err is human; to forgive, canine.
—Unknown

let's play

life's good

get lost

I'm scared

I'm cool

I surrender

canine glossary

bed boogie: circular "dance" performed by dogs before settling into bed, probably a primitive nesting behavior

copilot: dog riding in car, often with head poking out of an open window (*see also:* drool flag)

crazy mutt: exuberant greeting ritual

drool flag: visible tongue protrusion, frequently displayed during copiloting or meal preparation

FRAP: frenetic random activity period (*synonym:* zoomies)

full wag: the happiest tail position, a relaxed circular swish, sometimes including hip wiggles

fur on alert: raised hair on a dog's neck and back, an involuntary reaction often caused by fright or aggression

head tilt: quizzical look employed to charm gullible humans

LEAVE IT: the world's worst command, especially when applied to food

me-ball: dried excrement thrown at observers (*origin: Gorilla, informal*)

playbow: body position with elbows down and rear up, signaling an invitation to have fun

rhymes-with-pet-threat: vet, an otherwise kind human armed with thermometers and needles

tailspin: (I) chase involving the flexible appendage attached to the rear of most canines; (2) (*informal*) an embarrassing or quixotic effort

toe-twitcher: dream (often squirrel-focused) resulting in foot movement

tug-of-war string: a long (though never long enough) piece of fabric or leather used to lead humans during walks

UFO: (1) unidentified food object, often found under kitchen tables or couch cushions; (2) unidentified floor object, hopefully edible; (3) unidentified flying object, ideally a stick, flying disk, or slobber-covered tennis ball

water bowl of power: (1) jumbo-sized ceramic dish; (2) uncomfortable human chair, generally found in bathrooms

zoomies: sudden bursts of energy, usually involving chaotic dashes through the house (*informal; see also:* FRAP)

ONE

confession

Look, nobody's ever accused me of being a good dog.

I bark at empty air. I eat cat litter. I roll in garbage to enhance my aroma.

I harass innocent squirrels. I hog the couch. I lick myself in the presence of company.

I'm no saint, okay?

and while i'm at it . . .

I may or may not have eaten a pepperoni pizza with anchovies when nobody was looking.

Also, I may or may not have eaten a coconut vanilla birthday cake when nobody was looking.

Also, I may or may not have eaten a Thanksgiving turkey (except for the stuffing—*way* too much rosemary) when nobody was looking.

Nobody looking. That seems to be the common thread.

As they say on the crime shows: motive and opportunity.

robert

Name's Bob.

I'm a mutt of uncertain heritage. Definitely some Chihuahua, with a smidgen of papillon on my father's side.

You're probably thinking I'm some wimpy lap dog. The kind you see poking out of an old lady's purse like a hairy key chain. But size ain't everything.

It's swagger. Attitude. You gotta have the moves.

Probably I shoulda been named Bruiser or Bamm-Bamm or Bandit, but Bob's what I got and Bob'll do me just fine.

Julia named me. Long time ago. She's my girl. She calls me "Robert" when I get on her nerves.

Happens pretty often, to be honest.

numero uno

There's an old saying about us dogs, goes like this: *It's no coincidence that man's best friend can't talk.*

Lemme tell you something. If we *could* talk to people, they'd get an earful.

You ever hear anyone mention man being dog's best friend?

Nope?

Didn't think so.

Way I've always figured it, end of the day, you gotta be your own best friend. Look out for numero uno.

Learned that one the hard way.

That's not to say I don't have a best pal. I do.

Gorilla, name of Ivan. Big guy and I go way, way back.

Gorilla and dog. Yep, I know. You don't see that every day. Long story.

I love that big ol' ape. Ditto our little elephant friend, Ruby.

They're the best.

how we met

The first time I met Ivan, I was a homeless puppy. Desperate, starving, all alone.

It was the middle of the night, and I'd slipped into the mall where Ivan lived in a cage. I wandered a bit, grateful for the warmth, confused by the weird assortment of sleeping animals I found there, checking every trash can for anything edible.

There was a small hole in a corner of Ivan's enclosure. He was fast asleep, cuddled up with a worn stuffed animal that looked like a weary gorilla.

He was snoring, and man, that guy snored like a pro.

In his open palm was a chunk of banana, and—I still get shivers when I think about this—I ate it right out of his hand.

Guy coulda squeezed his fingers shut and I woulda popped like a puppy balloon. But he just kept on sleeping.

And then—more shivers—I am either a maniac or the bravest dog on the planet, probably a little of both—I hopped up onto that big, round, furry tummy of his.

That's right. I climbed Mount Ivan.

Crazy, I know. I have no idea what I was thinking. Maybe I was so exhausted I went a little bonkers. Maybe he just looked so warm and cozy that I figured it was worth taking a chance.

I did my bed boogie. Dogs don't feel right till we do a quick dance before settling.

Once I had things just so, I lay down in a little puppy lump and rode the waves on that tummy like a puny boat on a great brown sea.

When Ivan opened his eyes the next morning, he didn't seem surprised in the least to find a puppy snoozing on his belly. He refused to move until I woke up.

I think he was as glad as I was to have found a new friend.

the amazing history of
man's best friend

Before long, me and Ivan were best buddies.

We're an unlikely pair, sure. Ivan's calm and serene, a philosopher, an artist. I wish I could be more like that. No one's ever accused me of being levelheaded.

Hotheaded, sure.

And I can't talk pretty like Ivan can. I'm a street dog, after all. And proud of it.

Still, we clicked, in a way I never had with humans. "Man's best friend"? No way. "Gorilla's best friend"? You bet.

Seems to me the first time I ever heard that phrase— "man's best friend"—was while I was watching TV with Ivan.

Back in the day, Ivan had this little television, and we watched a lot of stuff together. Old movies, Westerns, cartoons, you name it. Poor guy was stuck in a cage, didn't have a lot else to do except throw me-balls at gaping humans.

Anyways. Me and Ivan, big fans of the tube. Cat food commercials. Pro bowling. *Dancing with the Stars.* What's not to like?

Once we watched this special on the nature channel. It was called *The Amazing History of Man's Best Friend.* Show was all about famous dogs. There were rescue dogs and therapy dogs and war dogs and fire dogs and movie dogs and this dogs and that dogs. And between you and me, most of 'em were just plain overachievers.

Then they got to this dog named Hach-something-or-other. Hatchet-toe, maybe? Seems his owner died (for the record, I object to the word "owner," but we'll set that aside for now), and Hach-something-or-other sat around for over nine years in the same spot at the same train station, day after day, waiting for him to return.

Thing is, the narrator guy was blabbing on and on about this dog, really over-the-top stuff: *How loyal! How loving! Break out the Kleenex! Blah blah blah, wah wah wah! Man's best friend!*

They made a statue of this dog. I kid you not.

A *statue* of the dog who sat around nine years waiting for a dead guy.

in my opinion

That dog was a ninny.

A numskull.

A nincompoop.

i'm yours

Lemme tell you about being man's best friend.

Being man's best friend can mean a lot of things. Companionship. Belly rubs. Tennis balls.

But it can also mean a dark, endless highway and an open truck window.

It can mean the smell of the wet wind as hands grab the box you're in with your brothers and sisters and you go sailing into the unkind night and still, still, crazy as it sounds, you're thinking, *But I'm yours, I'm yours, I'm yours.*

no one

That's what being man's best friend can get you.

A black highway.

An empty box.

And no one in the world but you.

early days

I don't remember much about my early puppy days. It was three years ago, but sometimes it feels like three hundred. Mostly I recall fighting with my sibs for the primo meal spot. Lots of squirming and squeaking. Everything soft and milk-smelling and movable. Like we were one great big complicated animal.

I never met my dad, and my mom didn't say much about him, except that he was trouble. Mom had a beautiful fawn coat. Chihuahua, some this, some that. Nice messy bloodline.

Mutts rule.

Mom crooned to us. Told us stories. Laid down the law.

I wonder if she knew she didn't have much time to prepare us for the world.

We were born in a dark place. Probably under some porch stairs, I suspect, since I remember the sound of boots plodding up and down, the biting and ugly smell of human feet.

They called my mom Reo. And they fed her most days, though sometimes she had to fend for herself.

She never showed fear toward them, or respect. Indifference, I guess you'd say. Unless they tried to handle one of us. She growled then, hoping to make it clear that we were hers and hers alone.

I myself got picked up a couple times. The hands reached in, grabbed. They were rough and smelled of strange scents, bitter and meaty.

My mom's growl made me fearless, and I wriggled and yipped. The hands shoved me back to the warm place, where I could sleep and drink and dream in safety.

Still, I understood, in my simple puppy way, that dogs belonged to humans, and that was how it would always be.

boss

My mom wasn't much for names. She'd had a lot of litters. I guess she'd run out of ideas.

My brother "First" was, natch, the firstborn. "Runt," my youngest bro, was the last. "Dot" had a little spot on her back, and "Yip" was always complaining. I was "Rowdy." Goes without saying. And that left my oldest sister. We all called her "Boss."

Boss was small but mean, with a distinctive sharp-sounding bark. She could outmaneuver any of us to the best spot for dining.

I admired her grit. Even if she did get on my nerves.

When we got a bit older, less blind, more cocky, I fought her off occasionally. But mostly Boss won. She was fearless, that pup.

alone

The truck happened without warning one night. They threw us in a box, left my mom behind. I can still hear her frantic howls.

I landed in a muddy ditch. It was a cloudy night, nearly freezing. Even the moon had abandoned me.

And the smells! Everything so wild and unknown. Animals with big jaws and bigger appetites. Birds that swooped in to kill. Death and life all mixed up together.

I searched for my siblings until the truth became clear:

I was utterly alone.

cars

The next morning I began my slow journey, moving through the tall, wet grass, my limbs stiff from the cold.

Now and then, I'd drink from a mud puddle or gnaw on some grass. By evening I was wobbly with hunger and thirst.

I followed the highway. Every time a four-wheeled creature roared by, I froze in fear. And yet—and this is what slays me—I knew that cars meant humans, and humans meant the possibility of living, just as much as they meant the possibility of dying.

the owl

Darkness had fallen when it came out of nowhere, the owl.

A shadow in a shadow.

They don't make a sound, you know. Not a sound.

It's quite impressive, when you think about it.

luck

Just as her talons, those marvelous weapons, raked my fur, I caught my right front foot in a small hole and stumbled.

If she'd gotten hold of my body, I wouldn't be here. But all she managed to do was grab my tail.

Only time in my life I've regretted my handsome hindquarters.

I was airborne, hanging upside down, dizzy and dazed. And just crazy enough to think, *Hey, I'm actually flying*, before the terror hit full force.

I caught a whiff of other animals below. Later I found out they were pocket gophers, but back then I just knew I was smelling something completely foreign.

The owl must have decided the gophers would make a more satisfying meal. She let loose her grip, and I plummeted to the earth.

more luck

Maybe it was my puppy fat, or my soft bones, or my incredible good fortune.

But I didn't die.

Didn't even break anything.

I'd flown twice in my short life and lived to tell the tale.

will

I found a small hollow at the base of a fallen tree. Poked my nose in and got a swat and hiss from a grouchy raccoon.

Kept going. Waddling, whimpering.

Lights ahead. New, strange smells.

Kept going.

Kept going.

It's amazing how much the sheer will not to die can keep you moving.

exit 8

I finally came to a small road curving off the main highway. Exit 8, turned out to be. A big billboard overhead had a picture of a terrifying animal on it.

Course I didn't know what a billboard was. Didn't know that the scary animal was a gorilla, let alone that he would become my dearest friend.

But something told me to follow the off-ramp.

And eventually I ended up at the Exit 8 Big Top Mall and Video Arcade, Home of the One and Only Ivan.

history

I made it to the mall. Slept in dirty hay by some garbage bins. The next night, I found that hole in Ivan's
cage. Stole his banana. Slept on his belly. And the rest,
as they say, is history.

For two years, I lived at that seedy old place that was
part mall, part circus, and all crummy.

But that was nothing compared to Ivan. He spent
twenty-seven lousy years there. And our dear friend
Stella, an old circus elephant, was stuck there for most
of her life, too.

When Stella passed away, it nearly broke Ivan's heart.
I tried like crazy to get him through those dark days.
But what really saved him, I think, was Ruby, our baby
elephant friend.

Before Stella died, Ivan promised her he'd get Ruby

outa that awful place. And to my amazement, he actually pulled it off.

Ivan and Ruby and a bunch of our other pals ended up going to different places, zoos and sanctuaries that knew how to take care of them. They're with others of their own kind. And they're loved and well cared for. It's been over a year now since we all moved, and they seem so much happier.

Me, I lucked out. My girl, Julia, whose dad had worked at the mall, decided her family needed a dog. Who was I to argue? Two square meals, my own bed, all the belly rubs I could beg for. What dog in his right mind would say no to that?

The best part is, we don't live far from Ivan and Ruby. I get to see 'em all the time.

I'm glad they're nearby. And I'm thrilled they've settled in so well. Really. It's a solid solution.

But it's not a perfect one.

tennis ball

The way I understand things, it's like this. We live on a lonely ball called Earth, and humans have basically been throwing it against the wall for so long that the poor ol' ball is falling apart.

It's like me with a tennis ball, chewing away until it's nothing but pieces of slimy rubber that taste like, well, slimy rubber.

And that means there aren't as many places left for wild animals.

Seems there are good zoos and bad zoos and good sanctuaries and bad sanctuaries, just like there are good dog families and bad dog families. The good places are trying to keep wild species healthy and safe. They don't want endangered animals to go away forever.

They also don't want the Earth to turn into a slimy, dilapidated tennis ball.

Although honestly, slimy rubber doesn't taste half bad.

You should try it sometime.

The thing is, I would give anything to see my dear pal Ivan deep in the jungles of Africa, where he was born. Or to see Ruby running across the savanna with a herd of elephants, her big ol' ears flapping in the wind.

I'd give up a mile-high pile of bacon cheeseburgers to see that happen. I really would.

But it ain't happening. I get that, and so do they.

When you're an animal, it helps to be a realist.

TWO

dream

This morning I wake up in my cozy bed, way too early for Julia to make me breakfast. She and her mom and dad are still asleep, and even the guinea pigs are silent. My belly grumbles, and once again I curse my thumblessness.

Humans are one big design flaw. The inferior noses. The inscrutable, humdrum rumps. And don't get me started on their—ahem—odor. But the opposable thumb idea? Yeah, that was a nice upgrade.

The cans I could open! The doorknobs I could conquer!

Anyways. I feel worried. Off.

Worry's a waste of time. And it doesn't fit with my tough-guy act. But sometimes I can't seem to help myself.

Before I woke up, I'd been dreaming about Ivan and Ruby and Stella.

It wasn't a nice dream, a fun-and-run toe-twitcher.

Nope. This one was a nightmare. A bad one.

We were swimming, all four of us, in a black, raging river. For some reason, I was in the lead. And I kept looking back, telling them I was gonna save them.

Me. Save them. Two elephants and a gorilla.

As I paddled like mad, their voices faded. I looked behind me and they'd vanished.

And then I heard it.

A faint bark.

That bark.

I woke up then, like I always do.

I did an all-over shake, trying to toss off the stench of nightmare that clung to me like shampoo after a bath.

I told myself to chill. Get a grip. Stop worrying about nothing.

And yet, some primitive part of my brain—the wolf in me, maybe—is on edge.

A lot can go wrong in the moment left to chance, the blink of an eye, the bounce of a bone.

There are so many ways the world can find to fail you.

the smell of a storm

By the time everyone else wakes up, I've calmed down. But the wind outside sure hasn't.

It's an early-fall Saturday, gusty, with scraps of sun. Clouds bouncing off each other like bunnies in a basket. Messages on the wind pouring in from everywhere. From dogs making their daily rounds, from feral cats, from anxious raccoons.

Basically everybody is asking the same thing: *What is the deal with the weather today?*

I already know. Weather channel was on last night, with a screen full of big, white, cotton-candy-looking swirls. Julia's dad, George, has already taped up several windows. Sara, her mom, packed an emergency bag just in case we have to evacuate.

Another hurricane is on its way. Third this season. Not as big as the last couple, but slow-moving. I've seen the routine, know the ropes.

Once breakfast is done, I sit on the couch in the living room, waiting impatiently for Julia to come home so she can take me on our daily stroll. She has a dog-walking service, and she's out walking other dogs.

I get my own private walk, 'cause she's my own private girl.

I can practically taste the storm coming through the open window: the back-of-my-throat tingle, the metallic edge, the fizzy energy.

But it's more than that. It's as if the air is up to no good, sneaking up on the world and looking for trouble.

on the poetry of stink

Of course, not everybody can smell what I'm smelling. My nose is a zillion times more powerful than a human's.

Dogs are experts at odor. Students of stink. We analyze the air the way humans read poetry, searching for invisible truths.

And we don't just smell the good and bad stuff that people notice with their substandard schnozzes. The usual suspects: popcorn and lilacs and freshly sharpened pencils. Diapers and brussels sprouts and freaked-out skunks.

No, our noses get it all, the whole shimmery double rainbow in April. Humans, they're lucky to get a cloudy day in November.

We get that molecule of roast beef dancing on the wind fifty miles from the tidy kitchen where it just slid out of the oven.

We get the cherry lollipop under the back seat of the Honda sixteen cars up on the highway at rush hour.

We get things humans can't even dream of getting. We're the ones who find the miracle earthquake baby cuddled in her crib under tons of rubble.

We're the ones who find lost hikers in the wilderness after a quick whiff of a sweaty sock.

We can even tell when someone's sick. We can smell seizures and cancer and migraine headaches. Try getting your guinea pig to do that.

We smell feelings, too. Sad has a sharp scent, with an undertone of sweetness. Sad smells like being lost in a winter forest as the sun goes down.

And happy? Happy is the best, but there's a touch of wistfulness around the edges. Happy smells like bacon ice cream served up in an expensive leather shoe.

You're going to love every minute of it, but you know it won't last forever.

the news

Sometimes when Julia and I go for walks, I'll brake at a corner (corners are the best for fresh news), and she'll tug and say, *C'mon, Bob, there's nothing there.*

Oh, but there is.

Here's the thing about poop and pee. I get that humans are not into them. I see the bathroom doors shut tight. The embarrassed, downcast gazes.

You guys are totally missing out. There's a whole lot of info hiding in your average pee mail. When dogs want to share the latest gossip, we just wait until nature calls. You'd be amazed what we can learn during a quick bathroom break.

People read the news. Check the TV. Browse the web.

I linger over a fire hydrant and inhale the whole wide world.

My ears, by the way, are almost as remarkable as my nose. I pick up on all kinds of things humans can't hear.

What we do with our noses and our ears is kinda like taking a big ol' knot and loosening it up. Separating out the strands. Unbraiding things.

People smell a reeking pile of trash in a Dumpster. We smell a dollop of cream cheese, a hint of peanut butter, a smattering of Froot Loops.

People hear the roar of a crowd in a stadium. We hear a strain of whiny four-year-old, a whisper of worried superfan, a note of grumpy hot dog vendor.

Man, dogs are cool.

snickers

While I watch from my perch on the back of the couch, Julia passes by on the sidewalk. George asked her to keep her dog-walking route close to home, in case the weather changes.

She's wearing a shiny purple raincoat and leading three dogs: a goofy mutt named Winston, a timid dachshund named Oscar Mayer, and . . . *her.*

Snickers.

An old nemesis of mine, Snickers is a fluffy white poodle with delusions of grandeur. A big, snooty, pain in the puffball.

Ooh, that pooch drives me crazy.

Our mutual dislike goes back to my early days as a stray. Snickers was a fancy, pampered, sleep-on-a-pink-satin-pillow kinda gal. Her owner, Mack, ran the mall where I lived with Ivan and Ruby.

That's where I first encountered Snickers. She teased me mercilessly, and beneath the fuzzy facade, I always suspected there was a little, I dunno, spark there.

Anyways. After the mall closed down, Snickers, being Snickers, landed on her feet. Mack married an older widow lady with more money than sense, and she dotes on that ridiculous poodle. Mack's too lazy to walk Snickers himself, so he hired Julia to do it.

"Lookin' good, Snick baby!" I call through the open window, and she gives me her curled-lip, squinty-eyed face, which, come to think of it, is pretty much how she always looks.

As usual, Snickers is dressed to the max. She's wearing a pink poncho, a sparkly rain hat, and teensy pink boots.

"Those boots were made for mockin'," I add for good measure.

It feels good, giving her some grief. But before I can really relish the moment, another annoying acquaintance of mine appears.

nutwit

Nutwit, the gray squirrel who lives in the live oak in our front lawn, jumps to a lower branch, looking at me with barely concealed pity.

I hate pity. Especially the barely concealed kind.

"I don't know why you taunt her," he says. "You're hardly in a position to talk, Bob. You *are* Snickers."

"Come over here to the window and say that."

"So you can, what, drool me to death?"

"Are you aware that my best friend is a gorilla?" I ask. "You would make fantastic ape chow, dude."

Nutwit reaches for a dangling acorn and yanks it free. "I thought gorillas were vegetarians."

"Ivan eats termites," I say. "He might make an exception for you."

"Face it, Bob. You're soft. You're one step away from your own pink rain boots."

"He has a point," says Minnie, one of the family's guinea pigs, from her cage next to the TV.

"No, he doesn't," says Moo, her cagemate.

"Yes, he does," Minnie squeaks.

"Doesn't."

"Does."

"Does."

"Doesn't . . ." Minnie pauses. "Wait, you tricked me!"

The guinea pigs rarely agree on anything.

Nutwit leaps over to the window ledge, acorn in paw. He presses his tiny, twitchy nose to the screen. "You couldn't last a day out here, Bob. Some of us have to live by our wiles."

"Hey, I lived on the street longer than you've been alive."

Nutwit nibbles his acorn. He's quite the prissy eater. "Whatever you say, Bob."

"I say scram."

"Fine. Hint taken. Anyway, storm's en route. I should be stocking up on my nut stash while I can." Nutwit gives me a wise-guy look. "That's how we do it in the real world." He scampers off with an acrobatic flourish.

Squirrels never do a simple jump when a quadruple-backflip-cartwheel is an option.

"You're full of it," I say to nobody in particular.

"We're full of it!" says Minnie.

"Yes, we're extremely full of it!" says Moo, and they popcorn in agreement.

Guinea pigs hop up and down when they're happy. It's called popcorning. And it's totally ridiculous.

You're happy, wag your tail like a real mammal.

"I am not soft," I mutter, nosing my protruding belly.

I leap, with effort, off the couch. Then I head to the bathroom for a good, long drink from the water bowl of power.

spoiled

I know Nutwit has a point.

I've become a creature of habit, spoiled after a stretch of being my own dog. For a long time, I was Bob the beast, cunning and streetwise.

As a stray, I lived off leftovers at the mall while Snickers dined on her fancy-pants kibble. Man, how I loved that cotton candy stuck to the floor. The unexpected UFOs. The ends of ketchup-covered hot dogs, scattered under the bleachers like, I dunno, big toes or something.

Ivan offered to share his gorilla food with me, and Stella and Ruby were always ready to pass along a carrot or an apple. But I refused. I needed to stay in shape, stay tough, stay true to my wild nature.

Okay, so maybe every now and then I'd sneak a banana chunk from Ivan's breakfast.

But then things changed. I became civilized. Domesti-cated. A *pet*.

Don't get me wrong. There are definitely some perks. Julia, who's an artist, painted my name on a food bowl. She gave me this wonderfully mushy blanket, the kind where you can bed boogie forever till it's squished to perfection and you can curl up just so.

I love that blanket. But I simply cannot sleep without Not-Tag, Ivan's raggedy old toy gorilla.

Course, just when I get my blanket and Not-Tag imprinted with the right amount of Eau de Bob, Julia's mom does the unthinkable. Puts them in the washing machine and removes every last bit of . . . me.

There are other indignities I tolerate.

The daily walk on a tug-of-war string, after going stringless my whole life.

The attempts to train me. Like that'll ever happen.

The kisses and cuddling.

Well, the cuddling's okay, I s'pose.

But the kissing I just don't get. If you wanna kiss your dog, why not just give him a big old lick on the face and be done with it?

Anyways. So what if I've gotten a little spoiled? A tad soft around the edges?

There's a difference between being soft and being afraid. Being a coward.

another confession

Too bad I know the truth.

I'm both.

cricket bully

When Julia returns from walking her charges, I race over and give her a good ol' Bob-style hello. Lots of yipping and twirling, followed by some attempts to jump into her arms.

Humans love that stuff.

Julia looks at me sternly and says, "Robert, down."

I leap some more because I'm determined to convince her I'm incorrigible. Untrainable. It's part of my charm. My Bobliness.

"Down," she says again. From her coat pocket, she pulls out her little metal clicker, along with some treats.

I hate that clicker. It's meant to help train me. But it's like a cricket bully.

Here's the theory. I do something right, Julia clicks. Gives me a treat. The clicks tell me when I'm behaving, and the treats reinforce it.

If that happens enough, before your very eyes I'm supposed to transform into a Good Dog.

Well, I ain't that easy.

"Down, Bob." Julia tries again.

I want a treat, but not enough to cave. So I opt for a playbow. A compromise.

Julia sighs. "You are definitely a challenging student." To my annoyance, she puts the treats back in her pocket.

I think Julia may be onto me.

trust

A while ago, Julia got it into her head that I needed to improve my manners. We went to a dog-training class.

I wasn't really into the whole Sit and Stay and Do the Tango stuff.

The worst command of all? The truly inexcusable, only-a-human-could-come-up-with-it order?

LEAVE IT.

"Leave it" means *Walk on by, Bob. Sure, there's a piece of bacon just inches from your drooling piehole, but do me a favor and just pretend it's not there, okay?*

Uh, not okay. Where I come from, you never pass up a free meal. UFO drops to the carpet, it's mine. And I'll be chowing it down before you can say, *Where the heck is my meatball?*

Within minutes, I was accused of being an under-motivated student, which is totally unfair.

I am highly motivated.

Just show me some cheese, please.

Anyways. I may or may not have been a little unruly. Class-clown stuff. Tailspinning, a little random pee-ing, some zoomies, just for show.

"Class, you see that crazy dashing around he's doing?" said the teacher, pointing at me with an accusing fin-ger. "We call that a FRAP. Frenetic Random Activity Period."

She pulled Julia aside. "He's a smart dog," she said. "But he's messing with you."

Which was true. But I hated getting caught in the act. I'd thought I was more subtle.

"Bob needs to know who's boss," said the teacher. "He needs to see you as pack leader. Give him some time. I see this a lot with former strays. Takes them a while to trust people."

Like forever, in my case.

As we left the class early, I yelled, "So long, suckers!" to my classmates.

Couldn't help rubbing it in just a little.

my car thing

I s'pose the real reason for the training stuff isn't my bad manners. Although they leave a bit to be desired.

It's my car thing.

I've always had a hang-up about cars and trucks. Also riding lawn mowers. Go-karts. Anything with four wheels, an engine, and a driver.

Don't like 'em. Don't want to ride in 'em. Don't want anything to do with 'em.

Those copilot dogs with their heads hanging out the window, flying their drool flags? Boneheads.

First of all, it ain't safe. And second of all, bad stuff can happen after you climb into a car.

Take it from me.

When Julia and George and Sara realized I have transportation issues, they tried to lure me into the back seat of their car with treats.

But you'd be surprised how stubborn I can be.

I yelped so loud, the neighbors came running out to see what was happening to the poor little doggie.

Score one for the poor little doggie.

click

That's when they started clicker training me.

Click, here's a treat.

Come closer to the car, Bob.

Click, here's a treat.

Watch while I open the car door, Bob.

Click, here's a treat.

Come right up to the seat, Bob.

Click, here's a treat.

Come on in, Bob.

Bob?

BOB?

WHERE ARE YOU, BOB?

Yeah, it was like that a lot.

options

Still haven't been in a car—or a truck or a tractor, for that matter.

When I have to go to the rhymes-with-pet-threat, Julia and her parents walk me there.

They say elephants have long memories. Well, so do dogs, people.

It's not like I'm afraid. I'm just . . . exercising my options.

full wag

"Are you ready to head over to the park?" George asks as he passes through the living room. He's carrying two flashlights and a roll of masking tape.

"Yep," Julia says, and I do a head tilt to show I'm intrigued by the conversation.

The place where Ivan and Ruby live is called Wildworld Zoological Park and Sanctuary. But everybody just calls it "the park."

George works at the park as head groundskeeper, which means I've got some sway. And everyone who's employed there loves Julia.

"Gimme a minute. I just need to grab my coat," says George.

"Straight home after that, though, Julia," says Sara. "Just in case the weather gets worse. One minute the weatherman's saying we're going to have a little shower. Next minute it's the storm of the century."

Julia scratches my head. "I thought Hurricane Gus wasn't coming till tomorrow."

"Sometimes they change course," says Sara. "They can be unpredictable."

"You know," George says with a wink, "in the old days, they only named hurricanes after women."

Julia groans. "That is so sexist!"

"It's not just the wind that I'm worried about on this one," George says. "It's the storm surge that could be a problem. Flooding."

Julia tries to make me wear her mom's latest creation, a knitted dog sweater with *SECURITY* written on it.

Which I suppose is an ironic reference to my petite size.

I politely decline.

"All right, you win." Julia sighs. "Ready for your walk, Bob?"

At the mention of the word "walk," I go all crazy-mutt so it's clear I'm on board with the idea.

Humans love it when we get silly. I think they're so weighed down by people problems that sometimes they need to be reminded what happy looks like.

Julia attaches my string. I try for a little tug-of-war, but she refuses to buy it. "Let's go see Ivan and Ruby," she says.

Just hearing those names sends my tail into full wag.

good words, bad words

I've never met a dog who didn't get a big ol' grin on his kisser when "walk" slipped into a conversation.

Dogs understand more than you might think. The nature channel says we're about as smart as the average human toddler. Two-year-olds, my fuzzy rump! We're a million times brainier than some babbling rug rat.

There was a dog on that *Man's Best Friend* show who supposedly understood like a thousand human words. Border collie, I think. Those guys need to switch to decaf.

The narrator was gushing about this wonder dog, and I'm like, *Well, duh, brainiac, of course we understand people.*

Not everything, mind you. And some of us are more attentive than others. Depends a lot on just how interesting your humans happen to be.

Certain words will really cause our ears to perk up.
The classics: *Treat. Walk. Frisbee. Bacon.*

And don't forget the swear words: *Vet. Bath. Fireworks.*
Vacuum cleaner.

We *always* hear those.

clock versus moon

Julia and I wait by the front door while George says goodbye to Sara.

I think maybe the hardest thing for me about being domesticated—a "pet," if you insist—is that I can't control my own schedule. If I had my way, I'd hang out with Ivan and Ruby all day, every day.

Unfortunately, humans love their clocks.

Dogs, we use the sky to tell time, like any sensible creature. Sky says it's dawn? Time to eat. It's noon? Time to eat. It's afternoon? Time to eat. It's dusk? Time to eat. It's midnight? Time to eat.

Point is, it's always time to eat.

Dogs have a thing for the moon, too, like wolves and coyotes and our other relatives. No calendars for us.

Moon looks like a claw, moon looks like half a pancake, moon looks like a tennis ball. Moon looks like a claw again? A chunk of time has passed.

But humans, nope, that's not enough. It's not a chunk, it's a month. It's not just dawn, it's 6:32 a.m. on a Thursday, and boy oh boy, we'd better hurry up and go to school or the office, or change the baby, but who gives a woof about feeding the poor, starving, sad-eyed, grumbling-tummied dog?

After a spell, I got used to the comings and goings of Julia and her mom and dad. But it keeps changing. Julia leaves early for school and is gone most of the day. She returns home excited and energized, good scents mostly. But every now and then she comes back smelling a little like me after a visit to the dog trainer—battle weary and ready to crawl under the covers.

Sara, who was pretty sick for a while, is feeling fine again, thank goodness, but she went back to work and she's away all day, too. And George, who has a job at Ivan's place, works five, sometimes six days a week.

That means it's just me and the guinea pigs a lot of the time. I have a doggie door and an outside run, but it's not the same as touring the neighborhood with your person. Peeing without a potential audience is like talking to yourself.

Sometimes I'm the teensiest bit jealous of Ivan and Ruby. They always have someone around.

Which is crazy, I know. I'm free and they're not. But there it is.

Told you I'm not a saint.

the shelter

I know our route to Ivan and Ruby by heart, and I can't help tugging a bit, even though I'm not supposed to. It's been a couple days since I've seen my pals, and I need my friend fix like I need air and water and belly rubs.

We don't live far. Down to the end of the street, around a corner (good news source there), then a few more blocks.

When I walk Julia—well, okay, I suppose it looks like she's walking me, but I beg to differ—there's a place we pass that always makes me jumpy and bummed.

It's the animal shelter. And I know it's a good place. A space for pets who don't have a safe home of their own. When I was abandoned on the highway, just a few weeks old, a nice cage with a soft towel in it and a bowl of fresh water . . . well, I woulda given just about anything for that.

Still, when I walk by and hear all those desperate barks and meows and squeaks, it gets to me.

Sometimes having great hearing is a pain.

Thing is, I realize I have a home and the gang in there doesn't, and I try not to think about stuff like that, you know?

I mean, it's not like I can do anything about their tough breaks, right? And in fairness, maybe those animals aren't like me. I've always been a resilient, hardworking sort. Maybe some of those guys even made their own bad luck.

Don't get me wrong. I try to be a nice guy. I do what I can to make the world a better place, sure. Chat with the guinea pigs. Lick the strawberry jelly off Julia's hand. Do my wag-and-dance when the 'rents come home to make 'em feel good. You scratch my back, I scratch yours.

But it's like I said before. You gotta look out for numero uno.

Guess that's why the shelter harshes my mellow. It's just . . . you know. I'd rather not have to hear those guys every time I walk by. Makes me sad.

Reminds me of the bad old days.

droolius

I knew this guy, back when I hung out at the mall with Ivan and Ruby. Nice dog named Droolius. Basic mutt, maybe some Lab and golden in there somewhere. He'd done some hard time at a couple shelters. One of those dogs you knew had seen more than his share of the bad stuff the world can throw your way. One ear bitten off. Scars. A limp.

Droolius lived in his backyard. Winter, spring, summer, fall. Chained up mostly. Flies on his food. Empty water bowl way too often.

Still, he always had a nice word to say when I'd pass him on my daily rounds, checking out the neighborhood trash cans.

Once I saw his owner—again, that word!—step onto the back porch. Droolius was barking, but he had a good reason. A stranger had just passed by. Barking is what we're supposed to do in that circumstance, right?

Maybe he's the UPS guy, maybe he's a serial killer. I mean, c'mon, we're not the FBI.

So anyways. Owner came out, big guy, mean-looking, gave Droolius a hard kick with his boot, yelled, "Shut up, you fool," disappeared.

Droolius looked at me, kinda embarrassed. We kept talking. A few minutes later, the owner came out again. Put some towels on a line.

Droolius headed over, tail between his legs, cowering, saying, *I'm sorry I love you I am yours yours yours* with his whole dog being.

Guy completely ignored him, headed back inside.

"He's having a tough time," said Droolius when the guy was gone.

"He's a jerk," I said, because subtlety is not my strong point.

"No. He loves me. He does."

"He has a funny way of showing it."

"Humans," said Droolius, licking a sore on his leg. "You know how they can be."

"Do I ever."

"But we gotta stay true. Love 'em. Forgive 'em."

I thought about that. Thought about it a lot.

"Why, though?" I finally asked. "Why do we have to forgive them?"

Droolius looked shocked, then confused. As if I'd just asked why cheese tastes good. It just *does*.

"That's the way it is," he said. "That's what we do, Bob."

I started to reply, but I managed to hold my tongue, which is not easy for me. It's a very long tongue with a mind of its own.

There was no point in making Droolius feel worse than he already did.

Later that morning, I found half a turkey sandwich. Gave the whole thing to him.

Well, okay, I had a taste first. But still.

forgiveness

Seems like forgiving humans is one of those doggie things we're all supposed to do. Like having zoomies or doing bed boogies.

It's written into our canine souls.

Well, somehow I didn't get the memo, the one that apparently went out to every other dog on the planet, about forgiveness.

Why should I forgive the humans who tossed me and my siblings out into the night? When you forgive, you lose your anger, and when you lose your anger, you get weak.

And when you're weak, you can get hurt all over again.

the art of human watching

By the time we reach the park, the sky is definitely in a bad mood. Gray clouds galloping like panicked horses. The nervous scent of rain on the way, the kind that makes you antsy in your own skin.

When we get near the employee entrance, I hop into Julia's backpack, like always. We enter through the special gate, where George shows his ID, checks in, and says hi to the staff.

Pet dogs aren't allowed at the park, natch. Foxes, wolves, jackals? My dog cousins? They are. But in my opinion, even though they're technically part of my extended family, they're nothing like dogs.

Only dogs have perfected the art of human watching.

The smartest thing we ever did was figure out how important the human gaze is. So often when we follow our owners' eyes, we're rewarded with something amazing.

A smelly sock!

A glazed doughnut!

A glazed doughnut that's fallen on a smelly sock!

We follow every blink, every sidelong glance.

We see it, whatever it is, before humans do.

We understand before they do.

And if there's a glazed doughnut involved, we eat it before they do.

puppy eyes

It's midmorning, still pretty early. There aren't many visitors around yet. "We've got a meeting in twenty," George tells a couple workers, Hank and Sonia, who groan. "Just a quick one. Going over contingency plans one last time, in case there's any flooding."

During the last hurricane, a small part of the park flooded, mostly near Reptileville. George helped move cages. He came home smelling like cottonmouths and copperheads. It was all I could do not to barf.

"Weather service just issued a tornado watch," Hank says.

"I thought we were having a hurricane," Julia says.

"We are. Gus. But sometimes tornadoes are spawned during hurricanes," George explains.

Julia frowns. "But a watch means 'maybe,' not 'for sure,' right?"

"Yeah, but I want you to head home," George says, "just in case."

"Please, Dad? Just ten minutes?" Julia says. She's using the special voice she reserves for moments when she really, really wants something from her parents.

I guess kids manipulate their moms and dads the same way dogs manipulate humans.

"I don't know—" George begins.

"I promised Bob."

I figure that's my cue to pop my head out and look adorable. So I do.

"Hey, Bob," says Hank. Sonia reaches over and scratches my ears.

I'm pretty popular around the park.

I give George my best puppy eyes, and he caves.

"Ten minutes, tops," he says. "Meet me back here."

Puppy eyes.

Works every time.

mr. oog

Here's how I figure puppy eyes got their start.

Cave humans were sitting around a fire, wearing mammoth fur and grunting about how there was nothing on TV because TV hadn't been invented yet, and some wily wolf thought, *Whoa, they've got leftover mammoth meat!*

And he probably whimpered and cowered and did a tummy display and looked pathetic enough that Mr. Oog finally tossed him a bone. And soon enough, a few zillion years later: voilà! Man's best friend.

After all that time, there's a thing, like a magnetic attraction, between dogs and humans. We've studied them for so long we can read every twitch and sigh.

S'pose it was easier than chasing down mammoths.

And I get it. I do.

The behind-the-ear scratch. The food in a fancy bowl. The bed by the fireplace.

Gotta admit that Julia's pretty fun to hang out with. And I'm grateful, really I am, that her family took me in.

Still, I don't *need* them.

You need someone, eventually they let you down and you end up feeling like a real doofus.

the park

As Julia walks, I sneak peeks out of her backpack, like I always do.

We pass the meerkat family, poking out from their den holes like the Whac-A-Mole game they used to have at Mack's mall. I see the flashy flamingos, with their one-legged balancing act. And the terrifyingly beautiful tigers. Even their cute cubs give me the willies.

Families, I've noticed, take a lot of different shapes. Jim and Joe, the penguins, adopted an abandoned egg, and they are the sweetest doting parents you ever saw. I see it with humans at the park, too. Families of all shapes and sizes and colors and genders and yep, they all seem to do just fine.

We round a corner past Sea Otter Alley. Oliver and Olivia are floating calmly on their backs, holding each other's paws. It's pretty adorable, I have to admit. But me, I don't need the trouble that comes with family.

Babies puking. Toddlers whining. Spouses nagging.

Talk about a design flaw.

change

The park's pretty big. Lots of twisty paths and fascinating smells. All the parts have names. There's the African Aviary. The Outback. Penguin Cove. Lemur Land.

It's like puzzle pieces of the world—a little Africa here, a little Asia there.

Dogs, you can find us pretty much everywhere. Our territory is Earth. As long as we're hooked up with humans, that is.

Along the shady paths, volunteer guides will answer your questions. They'll tell you about how animals used to roam one part of the world or another until things changed.

Things change.

That's one thing I've figured out. Don't ever assume a little patch of the planet belongs to you.

Things change. Boxes go flying.

my inner wolf

On our way, we always stop by the wolf habitat. Julia loves wolves. Probably because they remind her of me.

You have to look hard, maybe squint a little, but if you try, you can catch a hint of my inner wolf.

It's in the eyes, mostly. Also in my distinguished profile.

I dream I'm a wolf sometimes, and when I wake up, I'm panting and my fur's on alert and I'm feeling *Yeah, the world could hurt me, but I could hurt the world right back even harder.* Like there's a dangerous, hard part of me chained inside, struggling to go free and just, I dunno, get even.

Then I go see what's for breakfast.

kimu

There's a gray wolf at the park who makes me a little jittery.

Jittery, as in I sometimes worry he might like to eat me.

His name is Kimu, and we struck up a conversation when a mutual acquaintance of ours, a mockingbird called Mitch, introduced us one day.

Like Nutwit, Mitch likes to taunt me because I'm domesticated. Gives me a lot of grief about how free he is, soaring stringless over the whole town.

"I'm not the only one who's pampered," I said one day. "I mean, look at Kimu. He's not exactly running wild."

As soon as the words were out of my mouth, I regretted them. And when I looked at Kimu's *I could kill you with one quick bite* expression, I really regretted them.

"In any case," I said, moving the subject along, "I've lived wild. It ain't a picnic for a dog."

"What was it like?" Kimu asked. He moved closer to the edge of his domain. He had a strange odor, intense and scary and a little bit intoxicating.

"Well, I was just a pup," I said. "Abandoned by the side of the highway."

Kimu was listening intently. "Must have been tough."

"All I could think of was food, water." I didn't like the catch in my voice. "Owl got me."

"Those guys are fierce," Kimu said. "Can't hear them coming."

"I know, right?" I relaxed a little.

"I hate owls," said Mitch. "Hate them with a passion. They eat birds, you know."

"So do wolves," said Kimu, giving Mitch a meaningful look.

"So you were . . . wild once?" I asked Kimu.

"Never. Born and raised in captivity. Suzu, over there? She was. She's told us stories that would curl your fur."

"Honestly, it's nice to have a roof over my head. It's tough out there, man. Really tough."

"I suppose," said Kimu.

I looked at him and, for the first time, wondered if I really did have any wolf in me. He was a majestic animal, with teeth that could shred a tree trunk.

I am also majestic. But more portable. With teeth that could mangle a pencil with enough time and effort.

"Hey, Bob," Mitch said, "do dogs howl the way wolves do?"

"Of course we do."

"So let's hear something. A duet maybe." He fluttered his wings, revealing startling patches of white. "Do you know 'Talk to the Animals'? They play that on the carousel."

"Go away, Mitch," said Kimu, with just the right amount of menace in his voice.

"C'mon. Just a little howling. Pretend there's a moon. Pretend you're free. Pretend—"

Kimu growled, and so did I. His was pretty impressive. Guttural, deep. It spoke of death and dismemberment and all kinds of unpleasant bird nightmares.

I growled too. It spoke of . . . me being mildly peeved.

Still, Mitch got the message. He disappeared, a blur of wings.

"Actually, I've never howled at the moon," I admitted.

"Me, neither," said Kimu. "I'd feel kind of silly, doing it here."

enrichment

We're almost to my favorite spot in the park.

The great thing for me is that one corner of Gorilla
World juts up against Elephant Odyssey, the area
where Ruby lives. A low stone wall separates the
two spaces, and there's a moat on the elephant side.
The sections connect like two slices of pie, and my
secret spot is right at the center, where I can hang
out with my crew. Ivan and Ruby both have access to
indoor habitats, which is great when the weather isn't
cooperating.

The indoor space for gorillas ain't bad. I call it the
"gorilla villa." It has tons of ropes and hammocks and
branches to climb. Humans watch through a thick
wall of glass while the young gorillas run around like
kids at recess.

But whenever Julia and I visit, we can almost always find Ivan and Ruby outside.

We trudge up a little rise, though it isn't much of a hill. We live in a pretty flat part of the world. From there I can see just about everything: the park, the parking lot, the creek. Far beyond that, every now and then, I can even catch a glimpse of the ocean.

My secret place is a little hard to get to, right near the keepers' shed, nicely hidden by trees and bushes. Under a big magnolia tree there's a bench shaped like a gorilla holding out his arms. Julia likes to sit there and draw.

Sometimes she does her homework, which smells like frustration with a hint of eraser.

Whenever I visit, Julia props me up on the stone wall that separates Ruby's world from Ivan's. Visitors can't see me, and the keepers pretend not to see me.

If they caught any other dog there, he'd be out in a heartbeat. But Ivan and Ruby and I have a history. I make them happy.

I'm what you might call "enrichment."

At the park, they try to keep the animals engaged with surprises and challenges and changes to their environment. That's what enrichment is all about. The gorillas get watermelons to demolish and boxes to hide in and markers for drawing. The elephants get sprinklers and flavored water and elephant-sized rubber balls.

Not exactly like a day in the real jungle, of course. But the keepers try as hard as they can to make life interesting.

For Ivan and Ruby, I'm the ultimate enrichment.

I'm their best pal.

walls and bad guys

Julia takes me out of her backpack and I settle onto the wide stone wall. It's my fave place on the planet 'cause it means I can see Ivan and Ruby. But I also kinda hate it.

Walls will do that to you.

Ivan, being Ivan, is a mellow kinda guy. Takes the good with the bad, only gets angry when he really needs to. When I complain about the walls at the park, he says, "Walls keep the animals in. But they also keep the bad guys out."

Of course, gorillas don't have a whole lot of bad guys to deal with. Elephants either. So humans step in to fill the void.

Dogs? Sometimes it feels like we have enemies galore.

Everyone wants a piece of us. Humans treat us badly. Cars really have it in for us. We even get eaten by coyotes, which is kinda like having your cousin invite you over for dinner, then inform you you're the main course.

Although I'd probably just be the appetizer.

Anyways. After those twenty-seven years stuck in a mall, Ivan is one of those "glass half full" kinda guys when it comes to the walls surrounding him. Glad to be with others of his own kind. Cared for by smart and loving humans.

I'm more of a "water bowl of power half empty" kinda guy.

Every time I leave Ivan and Ruby, I am painfully aware that I *can* leave. Ivan's address is "Gorilla World." Ruby's is "Elephant Odyssey."

And me? I guess my address is the same as Julia and George and Sara's. 1249 Hinman Avenue.

I mean, of course it is. I've been living there a whole year now.

It *is*.

And yet, sometimes I still wake up at night and think, *Gotta find shelter, gotta find safety, gotta find somewhere to belong.*

Guess I don't want to get too comfortable.

gift

Once I'm in my spot, I don't have to do a thing, because Ivan and Ruby always know when I'm there.

Gorillas and elephants have great schnozzes, too.

Also, I pride myself on staying extra fragrant.

It's a gift.

ivan

Ivan gets to me first.

"Bob!" He knuckle walks up the hill—knuckle runs, actually—and he looks as glad to see me as I am to see him.

It seems like I've known Ivan forever. And yet every single time I see him I feel kinda awed. He's so powerful. So huge. Like this magnificent silver mountain that just happens to be my best buddy.

"Hi, Ivan!" Julia calls, waving. He cocks his head and makes a soft belch, which is gorilla for *I'm happy.*

Maya calls out to Julia from the door to the gorillas' indoor space. Maya's a zoologist, which is a hoity-toity way of saying she has a thing for animals.

It was Maya, and a lot of other good folks, who helped get Ivan and the rest of the mall animals moved to better places.

Julia unhooks my string and gives me a stern look. "No funny business, you," she says, and then she kisses me on the head. "And stay out of sight."

Ivan sidles up as close to the stone wall as he can get. "I was worried you wouldn't come today," he says. "Weather and all."

"Another hurricane," I say. "It's freaking everybody out." Above me, magnolia branches sway. Leaves rustle and shiver. Even the trees seem uneasy.

"What's new?" Ivan asks. He lies back on the grass and wriggles contentedly. Scratching an itch, no doubt.

"Not much. Had a weird dream last night." I pause. "You were in it, and me and Ruby, and Stella, too."

Ivan gazes at the darkening sky. "Stella," he says. "Now there was a great friend. Classiest elephant you'll ever hope to meet."

"The best," I agree. "I miss the old gal."

We fall silent. "All good with you?" I ask after a moment. No point in dwelling on sad stuff. Or bad dreams.

"Kinyani's getting on my nerves a bit. 'Ivan, do this. Ivan, do that.' But she means well."

Kinyani is Ivan's lady friend. Girlfriend? I've never been sure what they call it in gorilla.

Kinyani doesn't really approve of me. She thinks I'm a bad influence on Ivan.

I like to think she's right.

Ivan is four hundred pounds of pure power. But Kinyani is four hundred times scarier. Trust me. I've seen her in a bad mood. I've also seen her teeth. Make mine look like toothpicks.

Ivan and Kinyani don't have kids, but there are a bunch of baby and juvenile gorillas hanging around. They call him "Uncle Ivan," and he puts up with their antics.

Ivan's always been a good sport.

If I had a gorilla toddler hanging off me, I'd be tempted to use my toothpick teeth.

marriage

Ivan and Kinyani are a lot like George and Sara, as far as I can tell.

They grumble. They cuddle.

They help each other. They tease each other.

Sometimes it looks pretty nice. Still and all, when I smell love, I almost always smell worry. Seems like they're tangled together so tightly they'll never unravel.

There's a reason I avoid all that mushy stuff.

One big difference I have noticed between the two couples: Ivan and Kinyani enjoy eating bugs off each other.

George and Sara, not so much.

tiny but tough

Ivan always seems like nothing scares him. (Not even Kinyani, who scares the heck outa me.)

On the outside, I suppose that's how I look, too. Tiny but tough.

But inside? Well. Sometimes, no matter how hard I try, I can't find that guy to save my life.

It's like he's cowering in some corner of my heart.

I hate it when that happens. I hate that I'm not the guy my friends think I am. The guy the world expects.

I keep waiting for things to go bad on me. Worrying that my nice, tidy little dog life will blow up in my face.

I think George is a worrier, too. He'll get up in the middle of the night and head to the kitchen sometimes, his old slippers scuffing on the wooden floor. I always hear him. Always join him.

When he opens the fridge, the light spills out like maple syrup on a hot pancake. Wonderful scents drift my way. Leftover meat loaf. Stinky cheese. Expired yogurt that someone might as well eat, and it seems like the dog is the safest bet.

The smells rain around me, and yeah, my tongue starts hanging out, and I nudge George's pj'ed leg. "You can't sleep either, huh?" he'll say. Or maybe: "I can't tell if you have insomnia or just a very acute sense of smell."

Both, actually.

I wait. He usually makes himself a PB&J with banana, which is good with me, because the crusts are where you really get that fun chew factor going.

Now and then, after we eat, we sit on the back porch and George scratches my ears. Especially my right ear. It's my favorite.

I understand his worry, I think. George works so hard. His wife was really sick for a long time. And he loves his daughter so, so much.

Sometimes when Julia climbs on the school bus, I'll watch George watching her. All that caring and concern is painful to smell. Especially the briny scent of the stray tear he'll flick aside with the back of his hand like sea spray.

More than once, George and I have dozed off together.

That's the best kind of snooze, if you ask me. Good, warm, safe-in-someone's-arms sleep.

not talking

Often when I'm with Ivan, we don't even bother talking.

We just look out at his domain, at the green grass and the crazy babies and the swaggering juveniles and the hardworking females, and we think of nothing and everything.

When you've been through the worst with someone, you appreciate the best.

That's why sometimes, when he says, "Hey, Bob," it's enough for me to say, "Hey, Ivan," and then we just listen to the palm trees rustle and watch the saw grass sway.

brave

Once, when we were still at the mall, I told Ivan how brave I thought he was. The way he put up with everything that had happened to him and never stopped being a good guy.

Ivan just looked at me. Cocked that big ol' head of his. Nodded a bit.

"That's not brave, Bob," he finally said. "That's just knowing what I can't change."

"I call it brave," I said. "I call it crazy brave."

Ivan held a browning banana up to the light. Like it was the most beautiful thing he'd ever seen in his long gorilla life.

I wondered whether he was going to eat it or draw it. You never knew with Ivan.

"Seems to me there are lots of ways to be brave, Bob," he said.

A tiny mouse, name of Eek, skittered across his cage floor. "Hey, Eek," said Ivan.

"Just checking for crumbs," she said nervously, because she always sounded nervous.

"Dibs on all leftovers," I reminded her.

She looked so terrified that I relented. "Over there, behind the tire. Old carrot top."

"Respect, Bob," she said, scampering off.

"Take a small creature like Eek," said Ivan. He scratched his chin with the end of the banana. He did that when he was in a philosophical mood. "Maybe brave for a mouse is different from brave for me or brave for you."

He looked at me fondly. "You're the bravest dog I know, pal."

"I ain't brave." I chewed on my tail, avoiding his gaze.

"You are Bob, untamed and undaunted," said Ivan, and he chomped off a hunk of banana. He offered the rest to me, but I shook my head. I wasn't feeling hungry.

Also, it was mostly just peel.

"That's just my shtick. My routine." I hesitated. "I mean, sure, I'm tough, compared to, say, Eek. But that's setting the bar pretty low."

"You're too hard on yourself sometimes, Bob."

I met his eyes. He has these dark brown, deep-set eyes, really kind ones. Eyes that make you wanna admit things. Confess to your failures.

"Once when I was little. Just a pup. I did something . . ."

Ivan waited patiently. Ivan is the king of patience.

I felt myself dashing into a dead-end tunnel I couldn't escape. I didn't want to go there. Not even with Ivan.

"Never mind." I yawned. I do that when I'm anxious. "I'm rambling."

"Bob?" Ivan said. "You okay?"

"You know me, Ivan. I'm always okay. Always."

I slipped away before he could ask me anything more.

ruby

"Uncle Bob!"

Ruby races over—*galomph, galomph*—across the broad field that's part of the elephant domain. She's so cute when she runs, like she's determined not to trip on her trunk.

Ruby adores me. I make her laugh, I read the room, I lighten the mood.

I gotta admit, I *am* kind of adorable.

When I'm with Ivan, I think: *Pal, we've been through a lot, you and me. We are survivors.*

When I'm with little Ruby, I think: *Girl, look at you! Hard-luck past, and here you are, so much happier. So loved.*

Ruby, like Ivan, was plucked from Africa as a baby. She ended up in a circus that went bankrupt, then got shipped off to Mack's mall.

Ruby was taken in by dear old Stella. When Stella passed away, Ivan stepped in to play . . . well, elephant dad, I guess.

I did my part, too. Not 'cause I felt like I had to.

It just made life easier. Elephant toddlers are a handful.

You think humans are bad? Try putting a two-hundred-pound baby elephant in time-out.

ruby's family

Little Ruby seems much more content at the park, surrounded by her new herd. Old and young and in between, they spoil that adorable pachyderm like you wouldn't believe.

She deserves every minute of it. Kid had a rough start.

Seems elephants hang out in packs of females. Now that she's at the park, Ruby has adoptive sisters and aunts and grandmothers galore. (In the wild, the elephant guys head off, once they're old enough, and do their own thing.)

Sometimes I lose track of who's who among the elephants, because they're always taking mud baths, scrambling their smells.

By the way, what kind of animal actually *likes* baths?

Mud, sure.

"How's it going, girl?" I call to Ruby as she stops near the moat edging the wall.

"I had cantaloupe for breakfast, Uncle Bob! And it was yummy! And then I took a mud bath!" She pauses to take a breath. "Do you want to hear a new dog riddle, Uncle Bob?"

"Of course I do," I say, and I catch Ivan's amused glance.

"What kind of dog is always on time?" asks Ruby.

"Hmm. You got me, Ruby. I'm totally baffled. Befuddled. Bewildered. What kind of dog?"

"A watchdog!" Ruby exclaims. "*Watch*dog! Get it, Uncle Bob?"

"Not bad, Ruby. Not bad at all," I say.

"Ivan says it's going to rain buckets," says Ruby. She dips her trunk in the moat and blows bubbles.

"I think Ivan is onto something there."

"Did he show you his new picture?" Ruby asks. She grabs a tuft of grass and tosses it in the air. "I wish I could see it, but I can't 'cause of that silly wall. But he told me all about it."

My pal Ivan is quite the artist, just like Julia.

Ivan sits up and nods toward a spot on the wall.

"Another mud mural?" I ask.

As any good dog knows, dirt plus water equals mud, and mud means mess, and mess means let's roll in this stuff and maybe dig a hole or two or ten.

But for Ivan, mud plus a flat surface equals a waiting canvas.

I crane my neck, edging a bit farther down the top of the wall. Don't want to draw attention to myself.

"Hey, nice," I say.

I mean, I'm not an art guy. To me, art is a glop of spray cheese on a cheese dog with extra grated cheese on top.

Still, I've always admired Ivan's work.

"It's—" Ivan begins.

"No," I say. "Don't tell me. Lemme guess."

"You always guess wrong," Ivan says.

"Not always."

"You thought my palm tree was a dandelion."

"Art is in the eye of the beholder," I say.

"You thought my blackberries were giant ants."

Kinyani ambles up to join in the conversation. "And need I remind you that you thought his portrait of me was a chimpanzee with gas?"

"The resemblance was striking," I say.

Kinyani glares at me.

She glares at me a lot.

on the subject of chimps

Probably I shouldn't have mentioned the chimp angle.

Gorillas aren't as open-minded as dogs. A lot of them have a thing about chimps. Think they're clowns. But when I look at apes and gorillas, seems to me they have a lot more in common than they admit to.

Dogs ain't perfect. But I'll tell you one thing where we rule: tolerance.

For us, a dog is a dog is a dog. I see a Great Dane, I say howdy. I run into a puggle, it's *Glad to meet ya, how's it goin', smelled any good pee lately?*

Go to a dog park and you'll see. We are equal opportunity playful. You sniff my rear, I sniff yours.

You don't see that with humans, obviously. Constantly seeing differences where none exist. All those things like skin color? Dogs could care less. You think I won't hang with a dalmatian 'cause he's spotted? Or a shar-pei 'cause she's wrinkled?

I'm not saying I love every dog I meet. (Snickers comes to mind.)

But I'll always give a dog the benefit of the doubt. Life is short. Play is good. And there are plenty of tennis balls to go around.

a very handsome dog

"Hi, Aunt Kinyani!" Ruby calls.

"Once again, Ruby," says Kinyani, "I am not your aunt. I am a primate. And you, my dear, are not. More's the pity."

"But if Ivan is my uncle, then you *have* to be my aunt," Ruby declares.

"Ahem," says Ivan, pointing to the wall. "My painting, Bob?"

I consider. "It looks like . . . like a dog?"

Ruby flaps her ears. I can tell she is trying very hard to stay quiet.

"A very handsome dog," I add. "Is it—"

"It is!" Ruby exclaims. "It's you, Uncle Bob! Uncle Ivan told me!"

"But who's that?" I ask, pointing to another set of mud strokes.

"I thought you needed a companion," says Ivan. "I know you must get lonely at home, by yourself all day."

It's true. But I've never mentioned that to Ivan. Guy's like a mind reader.

"I think Snickers and Bob would make a cute couple," says Ruby.

I blink in disbelief. "Bite your trunk!"

Ruby starts to reply, but her voice is drowned out by a sharp clap of thunder.

"Storm's getting close," says Kinyani. "Ivan, dear, come on. You know how you hate the damp."

It's true. He carries around old burlap bags so he won't have to sit on wet grass.

Ivan looks at me sheepishly. "She knows me so well."

Kudzoo, one of the baby gorillas, bounds over and leaps onto Ivan's back. Ivan loves all the youngsters, but Kudzoo is his favorite. I think she reminds him a little of his twin sister, Tag, who died when she was still a baby.

"Ride!" Kudzoo commands.

Julia appears, her backpack at the ready. "Bob," she calls, "we need to get going."

"Ride, *now!*" Kudzoo repeats, yanking on one of Ivan's ears.

"Looks like it's time to go," says Ivan. "Good to see you, buddy. Stay dry, okay?"

"Will do, big guy." I turn to Kinyani. "Enchanted, as always, my dear."

A trumpeting noise cuts through the air. "Uh-oh," says Ruby. "That's Aunt Akello."

Akello, the oldest of the elephant aunts, lumbers over. "Come on, Ruby. Weather's getting bad."

"Just one more minute?" Ruby pleads.

"Now."

"But I need to tell Uncle Bob one more riddle."

"Now," Akello repeats.

"Nobody ever listens to the littlest elephant," Ruby complains.

"You can tell me the riddle next time, kiddo," I say, winking at Akello.

Ruby brightens. "Okay. Gotta go or I'll be in big trouble! Love you, Uncle Bob! See you later, Uncle Ivan and Aunt Kinyani!"

"I'm not your—" Kinyani begins, but Ruby is already galloping back to her herd.

the beginning

In the distance, thunder growls, long and low and not giving up. Reminds me of my stomach, pre-breakfast.

I test the air. Weird. Something isn't right.

"Julia!" It's George, rushing over. "Hurry up! You need to get inside."

George has an odd scent, like he's on guard. I've only smelled it a few times on him.

I look up. The clouds have turned strange shades of green and yellow and gray, clustered together like rows of fat marshmallows. It's so ugly it's beautiful. I can't stop looking.

The air goes still, like a cat before it leaps on its prey.

Kinyani and Ivan and Kudzoo are racing toward the gorilla villa.

A fat raindrop hits my nose. It tastes wrong. How can rain taste dangerous?

People are yelling, running. Opening umbrellas. Covering their heads with maps of the park.

More drops.

At the far end of the field, I can just make out Akello herding Ruby along.

Another drop. A dry one. Like a pebble.

"Hail," George says. "Julia. Now." He grabs her hand.

Rumbling. The sky boils and swirls.

"Bob!" Julia calls. "Come on!"

I move to leap off my perch. To run to Julia.

I've done it a thousand times. But this time, I lose my footing.

I never slip. I am as nimble as Nutwit.

But the rain, the hail.

I let out a yelp as I land on Ivan's side of the wall, splat in the mud.

"Bob!" Julia screams.

"He'll be okay," George says.

I can smell Julia's fear, and George's doubt, as he drags her away.

torn apart

Noise.

It's all noise.

Noise that hurts. Noise like a massive truck bearing down on us, the power of its engine, the inescapable wheels, the relentless roar.

Nothing to see, nothing even to smell.

Just the terrible sound of the world disintegrating.

no way

I'm flying.

airborne

Not far, just into the nearby giraffe domain.

Not high, just enough to buzz the tops of trees.

Not long, just long enough to stop breathing.

But I *fly*.

I'm not alone. Half the world seems airborne. Trees, boards, bicycles, chunks of roofs, umbrellas, chairs, bits and pieces of life: it all levitates past like some horrible magic trick.

Something hits my head—a toy truck, maybe?—and I yelp in pain.

And I'm terrified, so scared I pee myself, and I'll be the first to admit it—you try it and see how dry your underwear stays—but still.

I fly.

Not like in the box, the box with my brothers and sisters. Not like with the owl.

This is different.

This is me, Bob the dog, spending a moment as Bob the bird.

landing

It's over.

I land—*umph*—hard, on my rear, and slide to a stop directly underneath Stretch, the oldest giraffe in the place.

The roar—and by now I've realized we're talking a real, live tornado—vanishes as quickly as it came, leaving a vacuum.

A silence that hurts even more than the noise.

bad dog

And this is why I'm a Bad Dog.

Not Bad Dog, like I chewed your favorite slippers. Bad Dog, like I'm not a good representative of my species. Of any species.

I don't think, *Ivan! Ruby! Julia! Are they all right? I've got to find them.*

That's what a hero dog would do, one of those guys on the *Man's Best Friend* show. Hero dogs dash into flames and dig into rubble. Hero dogs are fearless.

Nope. Not my style.

What do I do? Bob, untamed, undaunted?

I howl like a newborn puppy.

honest

I'm not hurt.

Banged up a little, sure. But nothing major.

And I don't howl for long.

But it's what I do.

Like I said, I ain't a saint. But at least I'm honest about my failings.

stretch

Slowly, with some difficulty, Stretch peers down between his two front legs. His body partially shelters me from the rain. A piece of canvas has draped itself around his neck like an ugly scarf.

I swallow my howls. We look at each other, too stunned to form actual words.

Finally Stretch clears his throat. "Hello," he says in a strangely calm voice. "What kind of animal might you be, if you don't mind my asking?"

"Dog."

"Didn't think you guys flew."

"We don't. As a rule."

I pick myself up, move out from under Stretch, and take in my surroundings. The pelting rain has slowed some, and the wind has dulled.

"What *was* that?" Stretch asks, trying and failing to yank the canvas off his impressive neck.

"Tornado, I think."

I've seen tornadoes on the Weather Channel. They looked like water swirling down a drain. If the water were black and full of trucks and trees.

They looked like death.

I gaze up at him. I have to crane my neck. "You okay?"

"Yep," says Stretch. "But from what I can see, a lot of other folks aren't."

aardvarks

Across the way, I hear something.

A small squeak.

"Who lives over there?" I ask Stretch.

"The aardvark family," he replies. "Lovely neighbors."

Carefully, I venture across Stretch's domain. The sky is dark as dusk.

I hear a flutter of wings overhead. It's Mitch, the mockingbird. He's missing some feathers.

"Bob," he calls, settling on a fence post. "Was that you I saw up there?"

"Yep. How are things looking?"

"Not good. Lotta damage."

"Well, take care of yourself," I say.

"Likewise." He pauses to straighten a wayward feather. "Little hint, by the way. Next time you fly, try flapping your paws."

I make my way over a broken wooden barrier, tiptoe over some scattered glass and twisted metal, cross the paved path, and arrive at the aardvarks.

More sounds. They're coming from what looks like a demolished keepers' shed. I hesitate, not sure what to do. It's a big mess, and I'm a small guy.

Also, my head hurts. I feel dazed. Fuzzy. My ears are ringing.

I yank off some small stray boards with my mouth.

For the record, small stray boards have small stray nails in them.

Underneath the boards are three shivering aardvarks, two babies and a mom. They're strange looking, I gotta say, with their long piggy snouts and bunny ears.

"You good?" I ask.

"W-w-w-what was that?" the mother manages to ask.

"Some seriously bad weather."

"Is it over?"

I consult the wind. "Doubt it."

"You think everybody's okay?" she asks.

"Dunno. Sure hope so."

And then it hits me.

Ivan. Ruby. Julia. George.

"Look, I gotta go," I say in a strangled voice. "Any part of your indoor den survive?"

She nods. "Think so."

"Go there. Lie low."

"Where's Pedro?" the littlest aardvark asks.

I feel my head with a front paw. A nice bump is forming. "Who's Pedro?"

"Our keeper."

"He'll come," I promise.

"Are you sure?" the baby asks.

"I'm sure," I say, but of course, I'm lying.

sounds

The eerie quiet doesn't last. Before long, the squeals and shrieks and brays and squawks of the animal kingdom crowd the air.

Terror. Confusion. Pain.

From far off comes the wailing of sirens. Car alarms blare from the parking lot. Now and then, people shout.

Cries for help translate into any language, human or animal, fish or fowl.

Never want to hear those again.

Never, ever.

smells

And the smells! Like I said, feelings have a scent.

I figured I'd smelled pretty much everything there was to inhale in this big ol' world.

But the smell of sheer terror.

Of helplessness.

Of blood.

Of broken bones.

Of torn wings.

Well.

Turns out there are a whole lot of smells I've never encountered. Didn't know how lucky I've been.

surveying the damage

I pick my way past the devastation. The tornado has left a random path of misery.

The African Aviary is gone, simply gone.

The Kids' Farm nearby? Untouched. Although there are some very flustered chickens clucking like all get-out from the safety of their henhouse.

I see few people. Hopefully, a lot of potential visitors were scared off by the threatening weather.

It looks like some of the animals listened to their early warning systems—those little voices inside telling them something bad was coming their way. Quite a few seem to have taken cover before the brunt of the storm.

Wish I'd paid more attention to my own internal weatherman.

I pass the penguin viewing window, the one that allows visitors to watch their graceful swimming. Several penguins are underwater, swooping and swiveling.

"Joe! Jim!" I call, and they both swim over.

"Bert okay?" I ask.

Baby Bert pops his little head out of the water. "Hey, Bob! Did you know we're having a storm?"

"Yeah, I noticed."

"All good here, Bob," Joe says. "You?"

"Yep. Took a little flight, though."

"Daddy," says Bert, "can I fly?"

"In the air? Nope," says Joe. "You fly underwater. You're a penguin."

"Bob flew. And he's a dog."

"Bob is a very special dog," says Joe, and he gives me a look, a grown-up, just-between-us look, that says, *We're all right, but what about the others?*

baby sloth

I say goodbye to the penguins and continue on my way.
So much has simply vanished. Walls. Fences. Barriers.
Netting.

The orderly world of the park, with its careful lines
defining territory, isn't so defined anymore.
Many of the habitats are still entirely intact.
But not all.

What will this place be without fences
and walls? You didn't need to
watch the nature channel to
know that certain animals like
to eat certain other animals.

I pass two squirrel monkeys swinging happily from the children's
carousel. A pelican watches from
her perch on a popcorn stand.

I see a camel and a zebra together, looking stunned to be standing side by side.

I notice a red lemur, Merlin, on a picnic table. Lemur eyes are always big, if you ask me. But Merlin's eyes look like they're about to pop right out of his head.

I make my way through splintered wood and glass shards and approach the gift shop. It's roofless. Stuffed toy animals are scattered here and there like they tried to make a break for it. An *I LOVE KOALAS* T-shirt dangles from a tree branch.

Around a corner I see a baby sloth—Sylvia, I think her name is. She's resting on a muddy plush giraffe.

"Hey, there," I say.

She makes a tiny noise. A sloth sob, I guess it is.

"Let's find your mom and dad." I'm not one for hugging and licking and such, but I give her a little nudge with my nose.

Sylvia somehow manages to grab the giraffe, then looks up at me like she expects to hitch a ride.

How the heck do you pick up a baby sloth? It's not exactly part of my job description. And sloths are so . . . you know, *slothy*.

Carefully, I pick her up by her scruff, the way you do with a puppy. She puts that silly toy in her mouth, and off we go.

Takes a few minutes, but I find her mom, Selma. I deposit Sylvia on a patch of wet grass.

"How can I thank you?" Selma cries.

"No biggie," I say, and I head on, with fear in my belly and the odd taste of sloth fur in my mouth.

make no sudden moves

I've ridden around the grounds of the park in Julia's backpack enough to know every inch of the place. I've even chatted with many of the residents. But now everything is topsy-turvy. I keep finding myself in places I don't want to be.

Like the wolf exhibit.

Near the entrance, a sign lies crushed on the ground. It has a picture of a gray wolf with an arrow pointing one way, and another arrow with an emperor penguin on it.

To my right I see a piece of hay, stuck deep in a tree trunk like a pencil in a cupcake.

To my left, water gushes from a pathside ditch. A broken pipe.

The boiling sky has settled into a solid blanket of gray, and the rain's quieted to a steady drizzle. Still, I smell more bad weather menacing in the distance.

Tossed into a bush is a large informational display with a photo of two gray wolves. I don't see any fence or barrier or intact wall. And it dawns on me that grumpy wolves and tiny dogs might not make the best of pals, especially under these trying circumstances.

Just as I start to leave, a wolf on the sign seems to move. To blink.

Oh.

He isn't part of the sign. He's *next to* the sign.

It's Kimu.

"Hey," I say.

No answer.

Something tells me I should hightail it outa there.
Something else is saying, *Make no sudden moves.*

I hate it when my brain disagrees with itself.

I split the difference, crouching meekly. Doing the
whole submissive dog thing.

Kimu locks his gaze on me. I try not to make direct
eye contact. Lotta animals find that threatening. But
his eyes are mesmerizing. Glowing amber and way too
smart.

He moves again.

Two paws appear.

Big paws. Nothing like my feeble, shrimpy feet.

These paws are the size of hamburger buns.

Hamburger buns with lethal claws attached.

mutt versus wolf

I wait for him to launch into his pounce. Maybe if I
time my escape just right?

Yeah, sure. In a battle of Chihuahua mutt versus wolf,
even *I* wouldn't bet on the dog.

Do they break your neck before they eat you? That
only seems fair.

My heart's doing this crazy tap dance in my chest,
and I wonder if he can hear it. I sneak a peek at him.
Strangely, he just keeps staring at me.

Quickly I avert my gaze. Those eyes. Those chilling,
dangerous eyes.

"It's me. Bob," I say.

Kimu says nothing. He's panting hard. Maybe he's dis-oriented, even hurt?

I try to speak again. My voice seems to be hiding some-where deep in my throat.

Another try. "Um . . . Kimu?"

He blinks.

"Are you all right?"

No response.

"Anyone else hurt?" I ask.

This time he seems to hear me. "I don't know." His voice is a low whisper.

"Can I help?" I ask, really hoping the answer is no.

"Suzu. I can't find her."

"All right, then," I say. "I'll, uh . . . I'll take a look."

I poke around a bit, careful not to get too close to Kimu. A sour smell pours off him like sweat off a human.

"I don't . . . I don't see her," I say after a few minutes. "But I'm sure she's fine. Just a little shook up, probably. Hiding somewhere."

He doesn't answer.

"I should go. I'm, um, looking for some friends," I say. "Is there anything else I can do?"

He looks up at the ominous sky as if there's an answer waiting there.

"I don't know," he says. "I don't know. I don't know."

gorilla world

I move on. I have to find my friends. Have to. But where am I?

I leap over another mangled signpost with bent arrows. One way to Reptileville. One way to Lion Land.

I pass the Mangrove Swamp. A manatee pokes up her big head, draped with Spanish moss like a silly wig.

Two workers in yellow raincoats trot past me. One has a bloody bandage on his cheek.

I need to stop. Regroup. *Cool it, Bob,* I tell myself. I'm panicking, not taking in the right data. I try to blot out all the horrible smells, all the awful noise.

I concentrate, let my nose do the real work.

A whiff of something familiar. Gorilla? It has to be gorilla.

Full run now. I cut my back left paw on a shard of glass. Trip. Fall hard on my nose and cut it, too.

Dripping blood, I carry on. *Find them. Find them. Find them.*

A massive old oak lies on its side at the entrance to Gorilla World. Huge tangled roots grope into the air like frozen snakes.

And just beyond, where Ivan lives, is nothing but devastation.

help us!

The stone wall separating Gorilla World and Elephant Odyssey is gone. Pieces of both domains mingle: an elephant toy here, a gorilla nest there. Part of the indoor gorilla space has crumbled to the ground.

I scan the area where Ruby and her herd like to hang out. Nothing.

No gorillas, either.

Out of nowhere, the rain picks up, coming sideways, blinding me. The wind howls like a hurt dog.

This storm isn't over, not by a long shot.

I leap over a pile of cement blocks, catch my hurt foot on something sharp, yelp, keep going.

"Ivan!" I call. "Ruby!"

Nothing.

I get to a slight rise, leap onto another overturned tree, and try to make sense of the damage.

Red and blue lights cut through the rain. Police, fire engines. Good. We need all the help we can get.

I take in several lungfuls of the hideous air. It's too wet, too full of conflicting odors, a mishmash of scents I can't decipher, especially with my busted nose.

The wind gathers speed, pushing at me with incredible force. Feels like it'll tear my ears right off my sore noggin. I can barely stay upright.

Wind like that, storm wind, doesn't carry scent. It obliterates it.

"Help! Help us!"

It's a tiny, desperate voice.

Maybe even Ruby's voice.

kudzoo

I pick my way through the debris, trying to lock on the sound. It ain't easy.

"Please help us!"

Climbing over the remains of the wall, the one I was sitting on what seems like moments ago, I find myself at the bank of the moat.

"Ruby?" I call at the top of my lungs.

"Uncle Bob!" The sound of my name cuts through the gloom like a shaft of sun. Ruby runs to the opposite edge of the water. She's maybe eight feet away, but I can barely make her out in the torrential rain.

"You stay there," I yell, trying to be heard over the wind. "I'll come to you."

I follow the bank until I come to a spot where several chunks of wall have tumbled into the water. Three careful leaps and I'm across.

Ruby runs to greet me. She wraps her mud-coated trunk around my neck, and boy oh boy, am I happy to see that sweet little elephant.

"You hurt, Ruby?" I ask. "Is everyone all right?"

Ruby sniffles. "Yes, but—come quick." She dashes off before I can ask anything more.

Five of Ruby's aunts stand by the elephant side of the moat. Each one has her trunk plunged deep in the dark, muddy water. They look like a bunch of kids trying to find a lost toy in a swimming pool.

It's almost funny. Until I see what they're reaching for.

A baby gorilla is in the moat.

The tiny gal keeps grabbing for a trunk to hold on to, then slipping free. Her terrified screeches fill the air.

It's Kudzoo. Ivan's favorite.

an idea

"I'm going in," says Masika, one of the younger aunts.

"Might make things worse," Akello cautions. "Displace the mud, pull her down toward the bottom."

"I could go in," I suggest, the words popping out before I can swallow them.

"It's more mud than water, Bob." Akello shakes her head. "You'll get as stuck as Kudzoo."

I don't exactly argue the point.

"I've got an idea," comes a small voice.

All the aunties turn to Ruby, and she looks startled to have their complete attention.

"A couple of us get on the other side of the moat," Ruby says. "Grab trunks. We'll make like a, whaddya call it—"

"A sling!" I exclaim. "A hammock, like the gorillas have."

"I don't know, Ruby." Akello sounds doubtful.

Kudzoo grabs for Masika's trunk with both hands. "Wait," Masika says. "Think I've got her this time."

Masika lifts her trunk with deliberate slowness, carefully trying to support the baby gorilla, but once again, Kudzoo can't hold on. She lets out a despairing cry.

Down she goes, lower this time, her nose and eyes just visible.

"Okay," Akello says, with a nod at Ruby. "Let's give Ruby's idea a try. Masika, Laheli, Elodie, cross over to the far side. Zaina, Ruby, and I will take this side.

All three elephants move with surprising quickness to the spot where I crossed. They gallop back until they're facing us.

It's strange to see them on the other side of the moat. With the wall destroyed, they're technically in Ivan and Kinyani's domain.

"Move down a bit," Akello instructs. "That way." She motions with her head. "We want to scoop her out, not push her down."

Three on one side, three on the other, the elephants reach out for each other's trunks, creating a kind of cradle.

"Okay, now," says Akello, "lower carefully!"

Down they go into the muddy water. Ruby nearly loses her footing, so I grab her tail with my teeth.

It doesn't really help, and she yelps, "*Ouch!*" but my heart's in the right place.

Kudzoo thrashes her tiny arms. "Stay calm," I call. Easy for me to say.

She looks over at me, and I'll never forget the fear in her dark eyes.

Then she vanishes below the surface.

team elephant

"Hurry!" Ruby cries.

The elephants bend lower, moving like a giant elephant shovel.

"Where *is* she?" Masika asks.

"Lower," says Akello. "Lower, sisters!"

"There!" Ruby yells. "No . . . wait! There!"

"Up!" Akello commands, and the interlocked trunks rise from the muddy water to reveal a tiny, trembling baby gorilla, sitting in their makeshift sling.

"Kudzoo," says Akello, "stay calm, baby. We're gonna toss you to safety, okay?"

Kudzoo gives a little nod.

"On my count," says Akello, "start swinging. One, two, three!"

Up and over go the trunks, and up and over goes Kudzoo. She lands with a little *plop* on the gorilla side of the moat, right next to Masika's rear legs.

"Good work, everyone!" says Akello. "And good thinking, Ruby!"

"Th-thanks, elephants!" says Kudzoo, wiping mud from her eyes. "That was fun. Can we do it again?"

Akello takes a deep breath. "Maybe later, sweetheart."

Quickly I make my way back over the moat. "Kudzoo," I say, "follow me. Let's go find your ape peeps."

"Can I go with Bob?" Ruby asks Akello.

Akello touches Ruby's back with her trunk. "I'd much rather have you stay here, dear. And it's '*may I.*'"

"But Uncle Ivan!" Ruby pleads.

"I'll keep an eye on her," I tell Akello.

"I'm going," Ruby says in her most determined voice. "Maybe I can help. I helped just now."

Akello hesitates but finally gives a slow nod. Probably she figures there's no arguing with Ruby.

She's right on that one.

Ruby crosses the moat and joins Kudzoo and me. "Be careful," Akello warns. "There's more of this storm coming."

"I got her, Akello," I say.

"You'd *better* have her," she warns.

"I think I flew, Bob," says Kudzoo as we weave our way

through the wasteland that was Gorilla World.

"Yeah, me too," I say. "It's that kinda day."

what's out there

A handful of humans—firefighters and police, mostly—have begun to roam the grounds, checking out the damage. We pass a park employee with a weapon slung over his shoulder and a net in one hand.

"Tranq gun," he tells a passing police officer. "We don't know what's out there."

She nods. "How fast do they work?"

"On something like a big cat?" He shakes his head. "Not fast enough."

I look over at Ruby. "Stay close, kid."

As we near the gorilla villa—what's left of it, anyways— a screech hits my ears that makes the wailing police sirens sound like mewling kittens.

It's Kinyani.

She's frantically knuckle running back and forth near the collapsed gorilla villa. Chunks of cement, shredded wooden beams, and bent metal lie everywhere. A cluster of gorilla females and juveniles huddle not far from some rescue workers.

"There's Mama!" Kudzoo cries, dashing toward a gorilla named Jodi.

I'm so horrified by the destruction that I've almost forgotten my muddy little charge.

I really shouldn't be trusted as an ape-sitter.

Kudzoo darts over to her mother's waiting embrace. Jodi nuzzles her and strokes her and says soothing, motherly gorilla things. "Thank you," Jodi mouths to me.

"Don't thank me," I say, looking over at Ruby. "Thank this little gal. She figured out how to save Kudzoo."

"Thank you—Ruby, isn't it? Ivan's friend?"

Ruby gives a shy nod. "We all helped."

"I provided moral support," I add.

"I flew, Mama," says Kudzoo.

"Of course you did, dear," says Jodi.

Kinyani's fresh wails focus my mind. "I gotta go," I say. "Ruby, you should stay here." I'm going for a no-nonsense voice, the one Julia uses on me when she calls me "Robert." "Lemme see what's what. I'll be right back."

"No way, Uncle Bob," Ruby replies, just as firmly.

I give up. But I'm afraid of what she might see. Of what we both might see.

"Any sign of Ivan?" I ask Jodi.

She shakes her head, a grim look clouding her eyes.

With Ruby by my side, we approach the pile of wreckage that used to be the gorilla villa.

At the same moment, Ruby and I gasp.

There's Ivan's hand, barely peeking through the rubble.

not moving

I know that hand like the back of my own paw.

"No!" Ruby screams. "Uncle Ivan!"

I check the crowd. No sign of Julia or George. Nothing. No Maya, either, or other keepers I recognize. Just a few employees, several rescue workers, and two or three dazed-looking visitors.

"Is he alive?" a firefighter asks.

"Hand—whatever it's called—isn't moving," says another.

Weaving my way through the tangle of legs, I climb up the rubble pile, sniff a bit, and bark my loudest *Yes, he's alive, get your rears in gear* bark.

Just like those overachieving rescue dogs in the *Man's Best Friend* show.

I listen for a sound from Ivan, a grunt, a cry for help. Nothing.

Still, he smells alive.

At least I think he does. And that's good enough for me.

xena

Another dog races over, a tough-looking German shepherd wearing an impressive glow-in-the-dark vest and some bootie things to protect her feet from the rubble, but I hold my ground.

This is *my* friend we're talking about.

I lick Ivan's hand. His fingers twitch.

Well, that's all it takes to get both of us barking like maniacs.

More people gather. I see Maya next to Ruby, which makes me feel better.

"Name's Xena," says the shepherd.

"Bob."

I nudge Ivan's fingers with my nose. Nothing.

"And this is Ivan. My best bud."

"Sorry to hear it," she replies, and I don't like the sound of her voice.

With great care, and far too slowly for my taste, rescue workers begin removing chunks of the wreckage and tossing them to one side.

Xena and me, we mostly stay outa the way, but every so often I lick Ivan's hand, just so he knows we've got him covered.

I glance over at Maya and Ruby. Maya is wiping tears from her eyes while she strokes Ruby's ears. Ruby is giving Maya a comforting trunk-hug.

Good ol' Ruby. Wise beyond her years, that gal.

I check the crowd again. Still no sign of Julia or George. And that's when a sickening thought hits me like a bite to the belly.

What if Ivan isn't the only one under the rubble?

dragon

More police cars and ambulances arrive at the park. A handful of keepers stream in, too, looking frantic and confused.

The weirdest thing of all? Wandering through all the destruction are random park residents. Animals. Birds. Reptiles.

Residents who most definitely do not belong in Gorilla World.

A police officer is chasing an armadillo.

A great blue heron watches the mayhem from her position atop a giraffe statue.

A wallaby pokes his nose out of a bush, his saucer eyes catching the fire engine lights.

"Nets!" someone yells. "We need more nets!"

An older gentleman holding a blue umbrella lets out a bloodcurdling scream. "Dragon!" he cries. "I swear to you I just saw a baby dragon!"

"Sir," says a keeper named Malik, "no worries. That's actually a Gila monster. His name is Gilligan."

A paramedic raises his hand. "They have, like, venom, don't they?"

"They say a healthy adult won't die from it." Malik shrugs. "Although they'll be in some serious pain."

"Wonderful," the paramedic mutters.

I glance over my shoulder to see Sara running toward

Maya. I can't hear her words, but I can definitely see the worry in her eyes.

Xena's ears tip forward. "They're getting the cutters and the jaws of life."

"Jaws?" I repeat. Don't like the sound of that.

"Spreads metal. They're probably getting close. C'mon. We need to get outa the way."

"I ain't going anywhere."

"I hear ya," she says, and I can tell from the weary sound of her voice that she's had this conversation before. "But the best thing for Ivan right now is to let the humans do their thing."

I think about it. Figure she's right. I give his fingers one last lick. They don't move.

Nothing. Nada.

We pick our way to the bottom of the debris pile. "Hang in there, Ivan!" I call. "We love ya, buddy!"

I know it's crazy, but I listen anyways, hoping for a sign, any sign, that he's still with us.

hugging

I run to Kinyani. "Don't worry," I tell her. "He's gonna make it."

I can tell she doesn't believe me.

From there, I head over to Maya and Sara and Ruby. Maya has a radio handset in one hand and, for some reason, a young, squirmy meerkat in the other.

Sara kneels down and hugs me tighter than any sweater she's ever knit. "Bob," she cries, "what happened to your nose? And look at your paw!"

Some dogs don't like to be hugged that way.

I'm one of them.

But Sara needs to do it. I can tell somehow. So I let her.

Isn't so bad, really.

loose

A new police officer joins us. "Officer Williams." She nods at Maya. "You're with the park, right?"

"Yes. I'm Maya."

"This . . ." Officer Williams pauses. "We need to get this under control ASAP. Winds are gonna pick up, and we haven't even hit the eye. Storm surge could be an issue. This one's moving slow."

"We've got a skeleton staff here," says Maya as the meerkat attempts to eat her earring. "Early reports say maybe a third of the habitats are damaged or destroyed." She shakes her head. "We've got some injuries, some possible fatalities, too."

"Human?"

"Don't think so."

"Anything loose that could be a . . . you know, problem?"

Maya presses her lips together. "Yep."

"Such as?"

"A couple Florida panthers. Gray wolves. Python, maybe. Possibly an alligator or two. American alligators, not Chinese."

"I don't care if they're from Canada. If they eat people, we're in trouble."

"They don't. Typically."

"Typically," Officer Williams repeats. "Well, that's reassuring."

Sara loosens her grip on me ever so slightly. "Maya," she asks, voice trembling, "have you heard anything on the radio from George and Julia? I keep calling, but the cell towers are down."

"Nothing yet," Maya says. "But I'm sure they're fine."

"Nearest shelter's over at Lincoln Elementary," says Officer Williams. "You could check there."

Sara frowns. "They were probably here right before the tornado hit."

"We're searching the park, ma'am," says the officer. "We'll find them if they're here."

"Everybody, clear out," a firefighter with a megaphone yells from a spot near Ivan. "Could be danger of more collapse. We're working on this last metal beam."

I look to see if Ivan's fingers are moving.

Nothing.

"Hold on, Ivan!" I yell.

Nothing.

Sometimes nothing is the worst sound in the world.

Ruby lets out a little elephant cry, and then I realize maybe *that's* the worst sound in the world.

cpr

The wind dies down to a whisper, as if the world is holding its breath along with the rest of us.

"Do you have any vets standing by?" asks Officer Williams as two more ambulances screech to a halt nearby.

"Yes." Maya nods. "Not sure when they'll get here, though."

Officer Williams waves down an ambulance crew member. "You ever give CPR to a gorilla?"

"Primate's a primate, I guess," he says, but he doesn't look too sure. "What's going on?"

"We're waiting on equipment, but we're stretched pretty thin. Lot of structural damage on the north side of town," says Officer Williams. "They're going to get a chain on that last beam, try pulling it free with one of the cars."

"Somebody under there?"

"Gorilla, we think. Not sure what else. Or who else."

I look at all the cement. All the wood and metal. Nobody could survive that. Not even a silverback gorilla with the strength of eight men.

And yet. Ivan's fingers moved.

And then they didn't.

Several minutes pass. The rain slows a bit, along with the wind. The crowd watches as three firefighters attach a long chain to the metal beam next to Ivan, then hook it to a tow bar on the rear of a police car.

"Back up, folks!" calls the megaphone guy. "Farther!"

The chain clanks, the car growls, the wheels squeal.

Grinding. Groaning.

Progress. Just a bit.

The big chunk of metal has definitely moved a whisker or two.

More grinding. Wheels dig holes in the ground. Mud flies like thick brown rain.

A lurch. A snap.

Clanks and rumbles as the big beam jerks free.

The rescue workers move in, digging with their bare hands. Cement and dust and metal and bits and pieces of Gorilla World are everywhere.

But where is Ivan?

no

No movement, nothing.

But after a few more minutes, one thing is clear.

A gorilla-shaped mound has appeared. Covered by dust and dirt and debris and splattered with rain.

It just lies there.

I've lost a lot in my life.

My whole family. Stella.

But Ivan? No. It can't happen.

Not Ivan.

miracle

The mound sits up.

gorilla ghost

Ivan emerges from a cloud of dust like a jumbo-sized ghost.

He blinks several times. Coughs. Shakes. Stretches a little.

He's holding a banana.

Which he proceeds to eat.

Everyone, and I do mean everyone, cheers.

I scramble over to Ivan, and he gives me a look that says, *You're the best, Bob.*

"I thought you were a goner," I say, licking some banana goo off his chin.

"Me too." Ivan seems a little dazed. His eyelashes are white with dust. "What happened, anyway?"

"Tornado."

"Ruby okay? Kinyani? Julia? George?"

"Haven't seen Julia or George yet. Kinyani's over there, carrying on."

A paramedic holding a box of medical equipment approaches us nervously.

"I've got this!" calls a woman I recognize as one of the park veterinarians. The paramedic looks happy to step aside.

The vet gently but firmly pushes me out of the way. "I'll be back," I tell Ivan.

I run to Kinyani. "He's good, totally good." The look of joy in her eyes makes me want to give her an affectionate nose nudge.

Almost.

From there I join Ruby and Maya. "I was so scared, Bob!" Ruby whispers.

"Me too," I admit. "Me too. But he's fine. I promise."

We watch a pair of otters dart past, chased by a guy with a net. One of the firefighters who'd been clearing debris yells, "We're clear here. No sign of other victims."

Sara closes her eyes and I can smell her relieved tears.

While Maya listens to her walkie-talkie, trying to take stock of the damage to the park, Officer Williams's police radio hisses and crackles with new problems, new flooding, new dire predictions.

"Copy that," she says into her radio. Even with the chaos and noise, I'm close enough to the radio to catch the tinny sound of frantic barking.

"We've got a unit reporting the animal shelter down the street's flooding," Officer Williams says. "Also we've got trailer park damage on Twelfth Street, an oak down at Nelson Avenue blocking traffic, and a big rig overturned near the fairgrounds. And that's just for starters."

Out of the corner of my eye, I notice something airborne. It's graceful and bold, like a huge, wingless bird.

The crowd gasps.

It's Kimu.

He lands on the hood of Officer Williams's squad car. His eyes are glazed, his coat wet and shimmering.

"We've got a 10-91 here," Officer Williams whispers into her receiver. "Confirmed. Seems there's a, uh, wolf on top of my vehicle."

Slowly she reaches for the pistol on her hip. "Please advise."

shots fired

Several officers raise their guns. The tranquilizer dart guy takes aim too.

"No!" Maya yells. "No guns!"

Kimu blinks, eyes darting right and left, then leaps off the car with such grace and speed it's like he owns the wind.

Two shots ring out. Silence follows.

"Was he hit?" someone asks.

Maya closes her eyes. "I sure hope not."

"I sure hope so," someone else says.

jungle

As I watched that leap, watched Kimu fly, I didn't know what to think.

Part of me was like, *Go for it, dude.*

And the other part of me was thinking, *It's a jungle out there.*

a situation

Officer Williams climbs onto a picnic table. Someone hands her a megaphone so she can be heard over the din.

"Folks," she yells, "listen up. We've got a handful of animal control workers coming over, but several roads are already flooded out, and the weather guys are saying Gus is gonna take his sweet time. Meantime, park supervisors, call in more help, but only if your workers can get here safely."

The unmistakable roar of a big cat rolls over us like slow thunder.

"Any more tranq guns?" Officer Williams asks the park director, who's just arrived.

"Three in reserve," she answers.

"Nets?"

"We have a dozen."

"Okay, then." Officer Williams's radio crackles. I can hear more shouting, more barking dogs. "Shelter's flooding," she says.

"Yeah, that's happened there before," the director says. "Usually just a foot or two of water."

"Okay, public safety is where we start." Officer Williams wipes rain from her forehead. "We need to get the word out that these animals are on the loose."

"Of course," says the director. "We have protocols in place. But we need to be careful how we word this. People might overreact, might—"

"Ma'am," a firefighter interrupts, "I see a python in my backyard, I'm sure as heck gonna overreact."

"First things first," says Officer Williams. "Triage in the main office. Check wreckage for any survivors, human or animal. Fan out with tranq guns, get an inventory on how many animals are loose."

I wonder how it's possible that Officer Williams can seem so composed. The air reeks with fear, from animals, birds, people.

From me.

And yet she doesn't seem worried about herself. Just other people. Weird, the way some humans stick their necks out for others. Doesn't make a whole lot of sense, does it?

Again, the crackle, the hiss, the barking. My ears perk up for a minute. Was that a familiar voice? Maybe someone I know is in the slammer?

"I'm going to the shelter at the elementary school," Sara says. Her hands are trembling, but her voice is firm. "To look for George and Julia. Just in case."

She strokes my head and I'm happy to let her. I wonder if I should tag along with her, see if I can help out. Now that I know Ivan and Ruby are safe.

Hiss. Crackle. Meow. Bark.

I hear it again. My ears go on alert. My body goes rigid.

No. It's impossible.

never

Some barks you never forget.

one place

I know what I have to do.

Despite the turmoil all around me, the noises, the smells, the fear, the confused humans, the frantic animals. Despite my worry about Julia and George.

I know there's one place I need to be.

a split second

I want to tell Ivan and Ruby. But Ivan is still being poked at by the rhymes-with-pet-threat.

Although, come to think of it, she doesn't seem like much of a threat. In a movie, she'd be one of the good guys.

To my annoyance, Sara picks me up. I hate being picked up. Unless it's my idea. Then it's totally cool.

"Maya," she says, "you let me know, first sign of George and Julia, okay?"

"Promise," says Maya, and she places her hand on Sara's shoulder.

Humans, always with the touching. Although I kind of get it, under the circumstances.

"You can't take Bob to the school shelter. They're not allowing any more pets," Maya points out. "And the animal shelter is flooding, it sounds like. Why don't you leave him here? I'll put him in my office. He'll be safe."

No way is that on my agenda.

Sara nods. "Good idea."

She starts to hand me over but hesitates when she realizes Maya still has a meerkat wrapped around her neck.

It's just a split second, but a split second is all it takes to escape when you're Bob, untamed and undaunted.

on my way

"Bob!" Sara cries.

"Grab that dog!" Maya yells.

I spent a good part of my life running from a certain guy named Mack, and I still have my moves. I twist and spin and dip, and before you can say *Yes sirree Bob*, they've given up.

I backtrack, slip under a bench, and make my way to Ruby. "Ruby," I whisper, "I gotta go. Something important's come up. You and Ivan see if you can find George and Julia."

"I want to come!" Ruby says, stomping her right front foot in a huge puddle.

"You need to keep an eye on Ivan," I say. "Make sure Kinyani doesn't drive him loco with her sobbing. I'll be back before you know it."

I don't wait for an answer.

I'm off into the wild, into the world filled with wind and rain, with wolves and alligators, with a voice that could rip my heart in two.

THREE

looking

Ivan used to ask me what I did when I wasn't hanging out at the Exit 8 Big Top Mall and Video Arcade.

I wasn't like the rest of the animals. Caged, trapped.

I told him I was scrounging for food. And he never questioned it.

When you think about it, though, where's a better place to find food than the floor of a mall at the end of the day?

Yeah. I wasn't looking for food.

I was looking for her.

For Boss.

what if

At first, I didn't admit it to myself.

You know how it is when you wish for something so bad you're afraid to say it out loud, 'cause what if it never happens?

It was like that.

I knew the odds were crazy long. I knew I was nuts.

And yet.

I went out, day after day, searching for her.

six

There'd been six of us in the litter. So why was I only looking for her?

Because it was *her* bark I'd heard.

After the box landed. Even after the truck roared past.

I heard it. A whimper-bark-howl-cry, something I've never heard since.

She survived, at least at first.

I survived.

The rest of them didn't.

relieved

And what did I do, when I heard that bark? Did I run toward it? Did I try to find her, to save her?

No.

No.

I was just a few weeks old. Helpless. Useless.

The cries stopped almost as soon as they'd started. And you know what?

Part of me was relieved.

I didn't want to have to go back onto that highway. I couldn't bear wanting to rescue her and not knowing how.

I didn't want to see her die.

But mostly, I was afraid.

coward

I was afraid. A coward.

There's a certain freedom that comes with owning your faults.

the wind

Every day I went looking for Boss. Up and down that same barren stretch of highway.

Sometimes I'd catch a hint of something hopeful on the air and think it was my sister's scent. I'd be certain the breeze had brought me her voice, like an invisible gift.

The wind can really mess with your head.

enough

After a while I stopped going to the highway.

Stopped looking.

It was a relief to give up. I had enough to worry about.

my paddles

As I run from the park, I keep hearing my sister's yelp in my head. Still, with every step, my doubts grow.

Sometimes we hear what we want to hear.

The animal shelter is close, just down the street, but there's nothing quick about the trip. Water rushes past like a raging river. The sun's been swallowed by black clouds.

I pick my way through muddy front yards, avoiding the worst of the water.

I ain't much of a swimmer. Doesn't come up much in my line of work, though I do a passable dog paddle.

The problem is my paddles. My paws are tiny. Not much to work with when you're fighting a flood.

I see a couple humans with flashlights, carving tunnels in the sheeting rain. But mostly the street seems eerily abandoned, especially after the chaos of the park.

The shelter is at the bottom of a slight hill. Rain's pooled outside the front door, despite a pile of sodden sandbags. A police car is out front, parked at an odd angle.

I find some footing on a large rock near the door. Takes me three slippery tries, but I manage to leap onto the topmost sandbag.

I bark, bark with all I've got. But I might as well be voiceless, between the wind and the rain and the howling animals begging for escape.

inside

I pause to listen. I hear humans shouting, and I can make out what sounds like police radio chatter.

But I don't hear Boss. I'm right here, right at the source. Nothing.

It wasn't her bark I heard.

She's dead and I'm crazy and hearing things and drenched and shivering and where is Julia, where is George—

"Hey, little guy." The door eases open, just a crack.

Every bone in my body, every smart part of my doggie brain, says *RUN.*

This is an animal shelter. A flooding one, apparently. My sister isn't here. And I still have to find George and Julia.

The door moves.

Swoop.

The loop comes down around my neck so fast that for a moment I don't know what it is. It's like a cowboy's lasso, the kind in old Western movies I used to watch with Ivan.

But this lasso is at the end of a long metal handle.

And at the end of the long metal handle is a man.

"Stay calm, buddy." The man eases me, gently but firmly, off the sandbags and through the door.

I'm inside the bow-wow big house.

The hound pound.

The pet pokey.

Oops.

the return of snickers

The man pulls me along with his lasso. I decide not to argue.

We enter a small room stacked with animal-filled metal cages, and I'm assaulted by howls and hisses. The cold water on the floor sloshes as we walk, just skimming my belly.

As bad as my smeller is, I instantly pick up on one distinctive odor.

It's like the world's worst perfume, the kind old ladies emit. The kind people spray on their dogs to camouflage their lovely dog stink. The kind—

The kind Snickers wears.

I catch a glimpse of her in an upper cage. Bedraggled bow in her droopy hair.

"Snick baby, fancy meeting you here," I say. "You look good behind bars."

"Harebrain," she replies.

"Hey," calls a rabbit two cages down. "Watch your language."

"Mack couldn't deal with you?" I ask Snickers.

"He brought me here because he thought it would be safer."

"Seems he may have been mistaken," I say.

Carefully grabbing my scruff, Cowboy lifts me into an upper cage. He pulls the lasso loose and shuts the barred door. I'm not happy. But it's a relief to be out of my noose.

"Oh, great, another one?" calls a woman wearing tall rubber boots. She pauses in the doorway. "I thought we were turning people away."

"People, yes," says Cowboy. "But this pup came solo."

"Tick-tock, folks," says an older, ruddy-faced officer. He's holding a radio in one hand and a flashlight in the other. "You are running out of time."

"We hear ya. But first we've got to move everybody who's lower level." Boots sighs. "Last hurricane we had two feet to deal with. I swear they're getting worse."

"Climate change," says the officer. "What're ya gonna do?"

"More than we're doin'," says Boots. "That much is for sure."

"I'll move the dogs from room two," Cowboy offers. "There are only a couple on the bottom level. We're outa cages, though. We'll have to double up."

"Put that little female in with the new guy," says Boots. "They look like twins."

I'm shivering. And it's not because I'm cold.

I press my hurt nose to the metal bars.

I smell something. I do.

I hear something. I do.

Cowboy returns, dog in arms.

A bark.

That bark.

The door to my cage opens.

"Hey," I say automatically, even as my heart is already whispering the truth to me, "they call me Bob."

"They call me Boss," says the voice, but by now I know, of course I know, and I'm howling with joy.

alive

Thunder claps. Shutters fly. Windows rattle. Water rushes. Dogs whimper. Cats howl. People yell.

And all I can hear is my sister's voice.

catching up

We lick each other, sniff, yelp, circle, wrestle.

Neither of us was ever the touchy-feely sort.

But sometimes you just gotta let it all out.

"Wow," says Cowboy, watching us. "You'd think they knew each other."

tough

Boss isn't anything like I remember. She's scrawny and flea covered. Her left ear has a big notch in it. Her fur is dull, her body scarred, her tail cut short.

I'm afraid to ask how *that* happened.

She's clearly had it tough, really tough.

"I thought I heard your bark," I say, "but then it stopped. Figured I was crazy."

"I was napping."

"In this chaos?" I ask.

"I can sleep anywhere. It's a gift." Boss nibbles on a toe-nail. "Funny thing is I was having a dream about you. Must've caught a whiff of you in my sleep."

I can't stop staring. Boss. Here. With me.

"What?" she asks when she catches me looking at her.

"I was just wondering," I say, "about your life. Do you have . . . you know, anybody?"

"You mean like humans? Nope." She gives a little flick of her stubby tail. "Never have. Never will."

"You've been on your own this whole time?" I flash on my cushy bed, my lovely food bowl, the way everyone knows just how I like my ear scratches.

"Yep."

"How'd you end up here?"

"I was out scrounging for food. Just had another litter and I was tired, off my game. Animal control got me." She licks a nasty cut on her front paw.

"Wait." My ears prick up. "So . . . you have puppies?"

That would make me an uncle. A dog uncle, on top of being an honorary elephant uncle.

"Had the last batch seven, maybe eight weeks ago." She scratches at a flea.

"Last batch?" I repeat. "You mean you've had others?"

"Yep."

"What happened to them?"

"Dunno. It's not like they come home for the holidays, Bob." Boss lies down on the old towel lining our cage. "Or should I call you Rowdy?" She considers. "Nope. No, I like the sound of Bob."

"Me too."

"Anyway," Boss says, "mostly they're dead, I'd guess. You never know, though. Maybe a few got rescued."

She's so matter-of-fact. So resigned.

"This last litter, well, I thought I was onto something. Found this little car, you know those ones that look like a big ol' bug? Abandoned. Right down by the creek, near that bridge. Easy access through a hole in the floorboard. Blanket in the back seat." She pauses. "All the amenities."

"How many puppies?" I ask.

"Three. But only one survived, a male. The other two were pretty sickly, and, well . . . you know."

Something crashes into the front office. Sounds like a window has broken.

"We gotta get outa here!" an orange-striped cat howls. He throws himself against the front of his cage, then pokes out his paw, grabbing for the latch. "I'm too young to die!"

"When they caught me," Boss continues, ignoring the cat, "I barked for the puppy to sit tight, wait. Told him I'd be right back." She sighs. "Nice. Last thing he'll ever hear was a lie."

"What's his name? The puppy?"

She looks at me like I asked her if she's ever been to the moon. "I don't name them, Bob. Just makes it harder."

Below us, the water's slowly rising, filling the empty lower cages. We watch the humans rush back and forth, carrying buckets, as if they can stem the tide.

There's nothing to do. Nothing to say. And nowhere to go.

not right

I stare at my sister and try to imagine all the pain she's endured.

And here I thought *I'd* gotten the raw deal.

To lose your pups. To wander alone. To struggle for every drop of water, every crumb of food.

I mean, I experienced a little of that. But Ivan and Stella kept me going. And then Julia and her family.

Why me? What's so special about me?

Is it really that I'm more resilient? That I've made my own luck?

Am I somehow better than Boss? More deserving?

"It's not right," I blurt. "Not right you shoulda had it worse than me."

"Well, if you want to talk about 'not right,' you and I both had it a whole lot better than our siblings," Boss says.

"I will never forgive those people for what they did to us," I say through clenched jaws.

"Really?" Boss seems surprised. "If I held on to that much anger, I'd never get out of bed. Not that I've ever had a real bed." She sniffs at the towel beneath her feet. "This towel's kinda nice, actually."

I look at her in disbelief. "You're one of those? Those 'dogs must forgive no matter what' types?"

She almost looks amused. "Well, it is kind of our thing, right?"

"When someone does something hurtful, they have to admit it," I say. "Then they have to be punished for it. And maybe then, if they apologize and change, maybe—maybe—*then* they get forgiven."

"All I know is, I've done lots of bad stuff in my life, Bob. I've had to forgive myself plenty, just, you know, to get through the day." Boss gazes at me with her wise, weary eyes. "And I figure if I'm going to forgive myself, I'd better be ready to cut everyone else some slack, too."

evacuate now!

"Look," says the officer, "you need to evacuate now. It's mandatory."

"We can't just leave these animals." Cowboy sticks his finger in the orange cat's cage. The cat rubs against it, purring like his life depends on it.

Which it maybe kinda does.

The officer sighs. "You don't have a choice."

"We can't just leave them," says Boots, and I have to applaud her enthusiasm, even as I wonder why she'd risk her life for us.

There is no explaining humans.

"Just got word the bridge over Big Fork Creek collapsed," the officer says. "You guys gotta move."

Boots snaps her fingers. "Wait, you have a cop car, right?"

"Yes, I have a vehicle, ma'am," says the officer. "But the way the roads are looking, probably not for long."

"Okay," says Boots, "so we evacuate. We evacuate every last dog and cat and gerbil we can get in your car."

The officer purses his lips. "And take them where, exactly?"

"Shelter at the high school. That's where we've been sending people. They're not really set up for it, but once we started flooding and the elementary school stopped taking pets, they agreed to do what they can."

The officer grumbles, considers, goes for it.

The three humans load cats and dogs, parakeets and hamsters, one after another, into the police car. Some are in cages, and some, including a couple of unhappy cats, are on tug-of-war strings. Finally, it's our turn. Looks like there are nine of us left.

"Car's full and then some," the officer reports, struggling to shut the shelter's front door against the rising water. "We are officially out of room."

Cowboy looks at us, his eyes teary. "Don't worry, fellas. We'll be back." He sniffles. "I promise."

"You think we should leave the cages open, at least give 'em a fighting chance," asks Boots, "in case . . . you know?"

"Sure. But they couldn't handle this current. I can barely stand up." Cowboy shakes his head. "Look, I'll borrow my brother's bass boat. We'll come right back. Hopefully the water won't get much higher than this."

"Okay, then." Boots gives a grim nod. "Stay calm, friends."

Like that's an option.

preparing for the worst

The wind slows for a moment and the room goes silent. We stare at the black pool swallowing the cages below.

A chew toy shaped like a pink turtle floats past.

It's just us and a whole lot of water.

I check out the group. Two cats. One bunny. Six dogs, including Snickers, Boss, and me. There's nowhere to jump. No tables, no cabinets. No space above the upper cages.

And as Cowboy pointed out, the current is probably too strong for us to tackle, anyways.

"Folks, don't give up hope. You heard them," I say. "They're coming back for us."

"No way are they coming back," says a sad-faced beagle mix. "Gimme a break."

"You never know," I say. I am such a lousy liar.

"Oh, yes we do," my sister mutters, just loud enough for me to hear, and we share a look.

"Look, chances are the water won't get too much higher," I say. "But just to be on the safe side, pile up anything you have in your cage. Bowls, toys, towels."

"Who died and made you pack leader?" asks a big mutt with a graying snout.

"Well, it beats howling like babies," I say, and instantly I remember landing in Stretch's domain. Howling like a baby is exactly what I did.

"I had a dog biscuit this morning bigger than you," says Gray Muzzle.

"What about me?" someone squeaks. "Does the bunny get a vote?"

"Hold on, Thumper," says the orange cat. "This clearly is a job for a higher feline intellect."

"No!" A sharp voice rises above the din. "Listen to Bob. He's annoying. And his hygiene leaves a lot to be desired. But I've seen him get himself out of all kinds of scrapes."

"Thanks for the props, Snick," I say. "Especially the kind words about my odor."

The wind groans, and something metallic hits the side of the building. We fall silent again, waiting for more.

The windows rattle. The walls shudder. It's like the building is as scared as the rest of us.

"So," Snickers says, breaking the gloom, "you heard Bob. Start stacking!"

"How about my litter box?" asks a small, white cat with dark green eyes. "Would that work?"

"Sure," I say. "Use anything. The goal is to get as high as you can."

"And then what?" asks a young dachshund.

"Worst case, we swim for it," I say.

"That's actually *not* the worst case," says the bunny.

No one asks what is. We already know.

a question

We do all we can do. Which isn't much.

The rain hammers. The wind shrieks. Sirens come and go in the distance.

I wonder what Ivan and Ruby are doing. And what about George and Julia? Where are they? *How* are they?

Boss seems scary calm. Tough as old jerky. She looks the way I want to feel.

Before long, the water is lapping onto the floor of our cages. It's ice-cold. And moving quick. One inch, two.

Every now and then someone whimpers or moans. But mostly, we're quiet.

"If you can stand on your hind legs, guys, do it. Climb on anything you got," I suggest.

I turn to Boss. "When I say go, I want you to climb on my back. It'll buy you a little time, maybe."

"No way."

"Please. I need to do this."

Boss just stares at me. She's so thin. I can see every rib.

"To make it up to you," I add.

"What are you even talking about, Bob?"

I look away. "I'm sorry," I say, not sure where my words are taking me. "I could've . . . I should've saved you, Boss."

"Saved me?"

"The thing is . . . I heard you on the highway. And I should've—"

My voice trails off. I stifle a sob.

"Bob, we were puppies. Tiny puppies. Don't be ridiculous. How exactly were you going to save me?"

"I dunno. But I should have tried."

"We both did what we had to do." Boss nudges me gently. "Bob. This is crazy."

"I just . . . I can't seem to forgive myself." I whisper it, but I know she hears me.

Beneath the water, I feel a paw on mine. "I forgive you. Okay? Not that you need it, mind you. One condition, though."

I nod, wait.

"You have to forgive yourself, too."

Again I nod, and slowly but surely something fine and warm begins to fill my heart.

Before I can say anything more, Snickers calls my name. "Bob, dear? There's something I want you to know."

Boss winks at me. "Listen up, brother."

"Um, sure, Snickers," I call. "What's up?"

"Ahem." Snickers makes a little throat-clearing noise. "I've kept this locked inside me all this time, but now, facing the end, I feel the need to unburden myself."

"Really, Snick," I say quickly, "there's no need for that."

"The thing is"—Snickers pauses for dramatic effect—"I love you, Bob. I always have. I love the way your cute little tail gets all curled between your legs when you're embarrassed. I love the way you hum to yourself when you chew your kibble. I love the way you drool when you take a nap. I love—"

"I think I'm gettin' the picture, Snick. Thanks. That's awfully nice of you to say."

"And?" Snickers says.

Boss can't hide her amusement. "Go ahead, Bob," she whispers. "What can it hurt? We're all gonna die, anyway."

"Bobbo?" Snickers calls.

"Um, yeah. Yeah, sure. I, uh, think you're pretty swell, too, Snick."

"And what is it that you love about me?"

I close my eyes. Take a deep breath. "Well, um, those pink boots of yours, those are cool."

"And?"

I swear I'm trying, but I'm totally drawing a blank. In fairness, the water's up to my belly and my teeth are chattering so loud I can't hear myself think.

"And, uh . . . ," I begin.

"Oh, c'mon, how hard is it?" yells the bunny, who's perched on a pile of wet timothy hay. "She's a looker and she's smart and she's way too good for the likes of you. Try that, Romeo."

"You're a looker and you're smart and you're way too good for the likes of me," I repeat.

Snickers lets out a contented sigh.

"That wasn't so hard, was it?" Boss asks.

I groan. "Sis, you have no idea."

An awful noise comes, like a tree trunk splitting in two. While we watch in disbelief, a piece of the roof, the size of a Great Dane, simply vanishes. Rain gushes through the hole in torrents.

"Boss," I say, "it's time. Jump on my back."

"And that's a good idea because . . . why, exactly?"

"Because maybe you'll get your turn," I say. "Your chance to have things go your way. I've had an interesting life. I want you to have one, too."

"Bob, at best you're buying me a couple extra minutes," Boss says.

"Sis."

"I'm like thirty seconds older than you. You're not the boss of me."

"Please?"

"Why? Just because you're a guy? I could take you down in a second with three paws tied behind my back."

"And if you get outa here and I don't?" I continue, ignoring her. "There's a place I want you to go. Sit on the front porch. Wait for the humans who live there."

"Who are you kidding, Bob? We're both about to die."

"Three blocks up, four houses down on the left. Look for a big oak tree. Guy named Nutwit lives there."

"Nutwit." She's suppressing a smile.

"Say it," I command.

"Fine. Whatever. Three blocks up. Four houses down. Nutwit."

We go back and forth like that, arguing, bantering, trying not to hear the terror of our cagemates, and I think maybe I'm starting to hallucinate a little. I'm starving and freezing and I feel kinda dizzy. All the smells and sounds are mingling together, and, crazy as it seems, I actually think I catch a whiff of Ivan.

Well, that's kinda cool, I think. *At least I'll be remembering my best buddy when I die.*

There are worse ways to go.

hey

The water laps at my mouth, foul tasting and frigid. "Now," I say to my sister. "Get on my back *now*. I'm saving you, whether you like it or not."

Something in my choked voice scares her, I guess, because she leaps right onto my back with a horrified yelp.

I blink back muddy water. A silver presence looms before me.

Still, I'm not entirely sure it's him until I get a real big ol' whiff of banana.

"Hey, Bob," says Ivan.

giant monkey and sea monster

The screeches of terror are earsplitting. And my poor ears have endured plenty by this point.

"Folks!" I cry. "Relax! He's here to save us!"

"Monkey!" screams the orange cat. "Giant monkey!"

"I beg your pardon," says Ivan.

The bunny cowers in a corner of her cage. "If King Kong is here to eat us, I'd rather drown!"

"Sea serpent!" screams the beagle.

An arched gray trunk glides past.

"Ruby!" I exclaim. She's just tall enough to keep her head above the water.

"Ivan! Ruby!" Snickers calls in a delighted voice. "Over here, dears! Long time no see!"

"Hey, Snickers!" Ruby says.

Snickers wags her drenched tail puff. "My, how you've grown, sweetie!"

"Excuse me," says Gray Muzzle, "but maybe the happy reunion could wait till we're, you know, not underwater?"

Ivan taps his chin. He's always slow, always deliberate. I like that about the guy.

Except when I'm about to drown.

"We need to get all of you to higher ground," he says at last. "But the current's tough to fight, even for Ruby and me."

"There's always the roof," I say. "But it's damaged."

Ivan nods. "Seems there's a tree on it."

"Look, Uncle Bob!" Ruby says, paddling back and forth. "I'm an ele-mermaid!"

Kid always makes me smile. "Good work, Ruby!"

"I've got an idea," says Ivan. "It'll take multiple trips, so I'm going to start with the smallest creatures and work from there."

My sister gazes down at me from her perch on my back. "You actually know this . . . ape?"

"He's my best pal. Ivan and I go way back."

A long pause follows.

"Bob," Boss finally says, "you weren't kidding. You really *have* had an interesting life."

to safety

One thing about being a silverback. That strength-of-eight-men thing can come in handy.

Ivan starts with the bunny and the dachshund, one in each arm, along with the two cats perched on his shoulder and head.

One more trip, this time with the beagle and Snickers, and then Boss and me are on our way. Ruby holds tight to Gray Muzzle's collar and he manages to paddle alongside her, using Ruby as ballast.

It takes us a while to cross the street—the current's swift, and the water's up to Ruby's neck in places.

"Ivan," I ask as we approach the other side, "did they find George and Julia?"

"They're okay. A little banged up, but fine. They made it safely to a keepers' shed. Tree fell and blocked the door."

I choke back a sob of relief.

"George was out looking for you when Ruby and I left."

"How . . . how did you find me?"

"Ruby saw which way you were running," says Ivan. "And don't forget that gorillas and elephants have great noses, Bob. Maybe not dog level. But not bad."

"We followed your stink, Uncle Bob!" Ruby exclaims.

When we reach the far side, I see where Ivan has deposited our fellow inmates: the parking lot of a doughnut shop. The lights inside are off, like everywhere else, but I glimpse a few flickering candles, and people are milling about.

"C'mon, everybody," Ivan calls. "Let's get you inside. I'm hoping these folks won't mind a bit of company."

As we gather at the entrance, Boss pauses. "I'm, uh, gonna head out," she says, avoiding my gaze.

"What?" I demand. "I just found you! You can't leave now!"

She hesitates. "The puppy. Thought maybe I'd check. I mean, I know he's probably . . . gone." She looks at the muddy pavement. "It's crazy, I know."

"Yes," I say firmly. "It *is* crazy. Besides, you're too weak. And your paw is injured." My voice grows urgent. "Think about it, Boss. What are the odds he stayed in that car and waited for you? Who knows where he is by now?"

"Yeah." She looks defeated. "I suppose you're right."

"What's wrong, Bob?" Ivan asks.

"My sister—"

"Whoa! Wait! This is your sister, Uncle Bob?" Ruby interrupts, turning to Boss. "Then that means you're my aunt!"

"Boss had—has—a puppy," I explain. "Stuck in a car near the bridge." I point with my nose. Ivan doesn't know his way around town the way I do. "That way. Not far. She wants to try to find him, but, well, you know . . . he's probably long gone by now."

I know my words are harsh, but I'm trying to protect Boss.

No way that puppy is still alive.

Ivan strokes his chin. "Why don't we get everyone settled inside?" he suggests. "Then we can figure this out."

"Never mind," Boss says. "Bob's right. It's nuts. Way too dangerous. And probably too late, anyway." She takes a deep breath. "He's not exactly the first pup I've lost. You'd think I'd be used to this by now, wouldn't you?"

I don't know what to say. I want to make her pain go away. But what can I do?

I'm no bigger than Boss is, and certainly no smarter. And I've got my own problems. My busted nose, my aching foot. My angry stomach.

Look out for numero uno. That's my motto for a reason. It's kept me alive this long.

then, to my surprise

Some fool blurts, "I'll go find him."

And apparently it's me.

yay

"*We'll* go," Ivan says.

"Yay! More swimming!" Ruby cries.

"It's not safe, Ruby," I say. "You have to stay here. I promised Akello I'd watch out for you."

"I made it this far," she says, donning her elephant pout face.

Ivan and I sigh. It's exhausting, all this responsibility, this worry. This love.

"Promise to stay close?" I ask.

She holds up her trunk. "Elephant's honor."

"'Cause Akello will make dog soup outa me if anything happens to you."

"Yuck!" Ruby giggles. "Hey, did you know I can almost do a somersault in the water, Uncle Bob?"

Ivan taps politely on the door to the doughnut shop. But even a polite knock from a gorilla sounds like a visit from a wrecking ball.

The door opens a crack.

I think two or three people may have fainted, but we can't stay to find out.

I hop onto Ivan's shoulder, and the three of us head off. I glance behind me to see Boss standing on the pavement, watching us.

In the darkness and rain I can't read her eyes. But I'd like to think there's hope in them.

traffic stop

We slog up a slight hill and round a corner. The traffic lights are out, and nobody seems to be on the streets— that is, until we cut through a stand of palm trees and come across some police officers in a slow-moving squad car, its blue and red lights circling.

"Attention," one of the officers announces over a loud-speaker. "This area is under a mandatory evacuation order. Do not—"

The announcement stops, and so does the car.

"Uh-oh," says Ruby.

"I think they spotted us," I say.

"We're kind of hard to miss," Ivan points out.

The car moves closer, so close that I can see dropped jaws and bulging eyes.

The car brakes to a stop. The driver's side door flies open and one of the officers jumps out.

The other officer, a skinny young guy, follows suit, but he looks annoyed. "What are you doing?" he says. "Don't be a hero! We coulda stayed in the car where it's safe."

"I am looking," says the driver into her radio receiver, "at a gorilla and an elephant, and the gorilla has a tiny dog on his shoulder, and no, I have not been drinking."

"They said the park got hit by the tornado," says the skinny officer, carefully aiming his pistol.

"We can't exactly shoot a gorilla," the driver says, and I like the way she's thinking.

"Try me."

"What's his crime, exactly?"

"Jaywalking?"

"Thing is, I love elephants," says the driver. "My daughter collects stuffed elephants. I mean, you know. Stuffed toys. Not stuffed real ones." She listens to her radio for a moment.

"Get animal control out here," says the skinny officer. "Get a van. Get a moving truck. Get a 747, I don't care."

"Ivan," I whisper in his ear, "this is not looking good. You and Ruby gotta stay put. Don't make any sudden moves. No funny business, okay? These guys are freaking out."

Ivan sits down on the ground. Slowly. Very, very slowly. Ruby settles next to him.

The driver smiles. "Aww, that's so cute."

Skinny officer nods. "Yeah, in a deadly kind of way."

"I gotta do this," I say to my friends. "If you stay calm, they won't mess with you."

"But Bob." Worry clouds Ivan's face. "You need us."

"What I need is for you to stay alive," I reply.

I can see he isn't going to listen to reason, so I try a different approach.

"Ivan," I say, "it's like this. Boss is my sister. I let her down once, and now, well, I have a second chance. I'll explain it all later, but . . . I need to do this."

Ivan looks at the officers, guns drawn, then nods. "You are the one and only Bob," he says. "You got this, pal."

I leap into the air, into the vast unknown, just like Kimu did.

Well, maybe not quite so elegantly, but I do my best.

lightning and fireworks

It isn't far to the bridge. But far is relative when the wind is blowing down houses like the big, bad wolf.

I watch a stop sign fly past. I navigate around trees scattered like Popsicle sticks. I keep an eye out for gators and pythons.

Lightning strikes a tree. I brace for the thunder. It shakes the earth, the air, my teeth, my bones.

A branch falls on a power line. Sparks dance like fireworks.

I hate fireworks.

I move with more care after that. I know enough to stay away from downed power lines, thanks to the weather channel and *Storm Chasers.*

Man, I love TV. I'd give anything to be watching it from my nice, cozy bed right about now.

Good thing I know where the bridge is. My swollen nose throbs. What's the point in owning a top-of-the-line sniffer if it's not working right?

When I pass a bird's nest on the ground, I offer to help the owner, a jay. She swears at me. At least I think she does. I hear "nuts" and some other interesting words.

I tend to forget that in some circles, dogs are considered predators.

I wonder how Kimu and the other escapees are doing. One thing I know for sure, having been on the inside and the outside, is that way too much of the world ain't made for wild animals.

How would a meerkat cross a highway? How would a panther face down a city block? How would a wolf survive an encounter with a gun?

For that matter, who do I think I am, playing hero? Nutwit was right. I'm soft. I'm slow. I'm not a street dog anymore. I'm a pampered, lazy pooch.

I hear the rush of water, a different sound from the pouring rain, and out of nowhere, there it is: the creek.

Boss mentioned that the car was near the bridge. But when I get close, I remember what the officer at the shelter said. The bridge had collapsed.

And then I see it.

A little car, round topped, floating, caught in a dis-
lodged tree at the edge of the roaring creek, not far
from the crumbled remains of the bridge.

And on top of that car, even though it's completely
impossible, is a puppy.

Waiting.

And all I can think is: *That dog is a nincompoop.*

another bridge

The creek is filled with pieces of trees, boards, trash cans, plastic chairs, everything you can imagine. It's moving way too fast for me to try to cross.

I stare at the far side of the creek, at the collapsed bridge. I really wish I hadn't seen that puppy.

I know there's another way to cross the creek, of sorts, downstream a bit. An old pedestrian bridge made of wood and metal and rope. No one uses it anymore.

No one with any sense.

When I reach it, the little bridge is swaying like a cradle. It's blocked off by a rusty metal gate to keep people from using it, but I can easily squeeze through the bars.

I run halfway across, lose my footing, run some more.

Gulp. What am I doing?

A fresh gust pushes the bridge with such force that I slip. Half my body is dangling off the edge. I dig my claws into the wet wooden slats, and oh am I glad my nails are long and sharp because I fight off Sara's clippers whenever I can.

Pulling, pulling, pulling—man, I wish I hadn't eaten so much cheese over the years—and then *umpph*, one last effort and I'm back on the bridge.

It feels good, so good, to return to that little stretch of swinging slats. I want to live. Really I do.

I don't care about the puppy anymore.

I just don't want to die this way, not like this.

The fear's in my throat, my heart, my gut. I've gotta get off this rickety bridge, get back to Ivan and Ruby, back to my wonderful, Bob-smelling bed.

I'm not a hero, never have been, never will be.

I can live with that, 'cause at least I'll be alive.

I turn, moving snail-slow because the stupid bridge just won't stay put, crawling on my belly so I won't lose my footing again.

Almost to the end, I glance back, like a fool.

Just in time to see the car with the puppy lurch loose from its mooring in the tree, swirling into the middle of the creek like a toy boat in a bathtub.

The puppy isn't howling or anything. He's just lying on his belly, same as me, waiting.

What a nincompoop, I think yet again, and I'm honestly not sure whether I mean him or me.

hero

I will not lie. I am not thinking, *Oh yay, now I get to be a hero.*

Nope.

I'm thinking, *You have got to be kidding me! Just a few more seconds and I woulda been outa here.*

I may or may not use a few other choice words. Way worse than anything that jay came up with.

Then I run back to the middle of the bridge and wait a split second, maybe two, maybe three, and I jump.

cartoons

And I ain't proud of this, but halfway down I remember that I really, really, really don't like riding in cars.

I'm sort of dog paddling the air, thinking I can slow things down—maybe even reverse direction—like Wile E. Coyote in those old cartoons.

Cartoons are ridiculous for a reason.

not a movie

So in a movie, I'd land all graceful and tough and grab that little guy.

But this isn't a movie.

I kinda land on top of him. Legs splayed like a bug on a windshield.

Not enough to smush him.

But definitely enough to annoy him.

The car spins, dips, rights itself.

"Hi," I say. "I'm your uncle Bob."

"If you're my uncle, why are you trying to kill me?" he asks.

Pup has a mouth on him, for being so tiny.

"I'm saving you, dude." I grab his scruff with my teeth.

"Ouch," he says.

The car seesaws. I scrabble, clawing at the slick skin of the roof. My nails make a horrible scraping sound.

It's like trying to hug a whale.

"Can you swim?" I ask out of the side of my mouth. It's hard to talk with a puppy between your teeth.

"No. Can you?"

"Yes. But I suspect the degree of difficulty will go up considerably with a puppy in my mouth."

The car lists, recovers, lopes along like a jackrabbit in tall grass. My claws make tracks in the paint.

"How'd you get on top of the car?" I ask.

"Wasn't easy. Branch broke through one of the windows. I climbed out that way."

"Impressive."

"By the way," says the puppy, "I think we may be sinking."

"No kidding, Sherlock." I don't mean to sound unkind. I'm a bit stressed.

"I don't have a name, actually."

"How about Rowdy?" I suggest. "I hear it's available."

"Sure, what the heck? So what's your plan?"

"You tell me," I say. "What'd you think was going to happen?"

"I figured someone would come along and save me. Some human, maybe."

"Dog's best friend?" I say.

"If you say so."

Another lurch. We're going down.

"Hang on, pup," I say. "Man's best friend is gonna save you instead."

do not let go

The water's cold, so cold it burns. I paddle frantically. Nothing happens. It's like pawing air.

I keep my teeth tight on Rowdy. *Do not let go. Do not let go*, I tell myself, but the water's churning into my nose and throat, and if I cough, he'll be a goner.

We hit something hard and metal straight on. I'm underwater, submerged, as bits and pieces of the world rush past.

It's like the tornado, only wetter.

I dig at the darkness. I think of all the things I'll miss when I'm dead.

Cheese tops the list.

Well, okay, maybe Ivan and Ruby and Julia and George and Sara top the list.

But then totally cheese.

My back paws graze the bottom. My nose burns. My lungs burn. Everything burns.

I have to cough.

I can't cough.

Mustering all my strength, I struggle to the surface for a moment, fighting the water with my paws.

Rowdy is dead weight in my mouth.

I hit bottom again, and this time I use it like a spring-board, lurching toward the edge of the water, toward solid land, toward grass and dirt and trees and bushes and—

A whoosh of fur and pain, oh man, the pain, someone grabbing my paw, losing it, teeth, sharp, sharp teeth, the smell, even with my messed-up nose, of wildness and danger.

Something grabs my scruff, yanks, pulls me to safety.

Back to the world. Back from the brink.

kimu again

Kimu has me.

He drops me to the mud. His teeth smell of blood. My blood.

I drop Rowdy. My teeth smell of blood, too.

For a long time, no words come, just panting, coughing, panting some more.

Nothing from the puppy. I shove him with my paw, nudge him with my nose.

Nothing.

I look at Kimu, his fur spiked, his eyes wild, different, unknowable.

"I guess they didn't shoot you?" I say.

"They tried," he says, eyes on the puppy.

"Thank you for . . ." I trail off.

He glances at me. "Didn't do it for you." A pause. "Did it for me."

With his right front paw, he claws at the puppy. At Rowdy.

"Hey," I say without really thinking. Or registering the size of his paw. Or realizing that he's drooling, just a little.

"He, uh." I put my paw, my puny pathetic loser paw, on Rowdy too. "He's my . . . my nephew, and well, I—"

"Didn't take you for the sentimental sort, Bob."

"I'm not. Just, you know how it is."

"No, actually, I don't know. I'm a wild animal. Not a pet."

"Still." I clear my throat and remind myself that rolling over and peeing myself is not an acceptable option. "Still and all, he's scrawny, might even be dead, who knows? You got better breakfasts at the park."

I recognize all too well the look he gives me. The look of sadness and loss and anger, the look of someone who will never forgive the world.

He's running with the puppy dangling from his jaws before I even know what's happened.

how

I don't know how I do it.

If I did know, maybe I could understand that other part of me. The wolf part.

I run, faster than I've ever run.

I growl, louder than I've ever growled.

I grab Kimu's throat. I clamp down.

I do not let go.

gone

He can kill me. With a sidelong glance and a half-hearted bite, he can kill me.

I know that.

But he doesn't.

He drops the puppy.

He shakes me off and pulls free

He pauses. Looks at me like he's seeing me for the first time.

He gazes at the sky, thick with clouds. No moon. Barely any sun.

He raises his head.

His howl is long and sad and beautiful.

He runs.

first aid

Rowdy still isn't moving.

I don't know what else to do.

So I bite the heck outa his tail.

Perks the little guy right up.

the truth

It hits me then. I'm so tired. So banged up. I can't go on, even if I want to.

I carry Rowdy to a sheltering tree. Cuddle him close. Give him a couple licks for good measure.

"Now what?" he asks.

"Now," I say, "we wait."

"For what?"

"For humans," I answer. "For help."

"Are you sure they'll come?"

I think for a moment.

I remember all the people I've seen today, the police and rescue workers, the park employees, the staff at the shelter, the folks at the doughnut shop opening their door to a strange collection of animals. I remember George running to get Julia, and Julia trying to get me, and Sara struggling to find them both.

I breathe in the sweet smell of puppy. It's important to tell the truth.

"I'm sure," I say.

forever

The eye of the hurricane passes. The storm rages on.

It feels like a year. Like nine years, even.

It feels like forever.

rescue

When I hear Julia calling my name through the open window of her parents' car, I pick up Rowdy and dash over like it's my favorite place on this lonely ball called Earth.

No clickers necessary.

No treats required.

I fly my drool flag all the way home.

FOUR

aftermath

We've lost ten park residents total. Eight deaths, plus two still missing. No humans died, but there were some injuries.

They've already started rebuilding. It's funny the way people go right back at it after a tragedy. Everyone comes together. Lots of talk about community and *kumbaya, blahblahblah.*

They're a resilient species, I'll give them that.

It's been three weeks, and we still don't have Kimu back. Suzu either. There've been some sightings, nothing for sure.

I worry they can't last long. Wolves aren't native to this part of the world.

I like to think they're together, at least.

Everybody else is back, with makeshift domains. Nobody's complaining, though.

In spite of all the construction, Julia's been taking me to see Ivan and Ruby whenever she can.

Today Ivan leans on the temporary fence separating him from the elephants. Maya made him a medal for valor out of a watermelon and cucumbers. He's eaten most of it.

"It's pretty great almost everybody we saved from the shelter ended up with a home," says Ivan. "Even that annoying bunny."

"Almost everyone," I remind him.

"I'm so sorry about Boss," he says in his gentle way.

From what we can tell, Boss never went into the dough-nut shop. She slipped away, and no one knows what happened to her.

I try not to feel hurt. But I had this silly fantasy about me and her and Rowdy all hanging out together like a family.

And I so wanted her to know what it's like to have a warm bed and a full bowl and a good ear scratch when-ever you need it.

I wanted her to know she deserves that as much as any dog.

I guess she'd lived life too long on her own terms. Or maybe she was afraid to get her hopes up. To trust.

I understand. Been there, done that.

But sometimes humans don't let you down. Sometimes they even come to the rescue.

riddle

"Uncle Bob!" Ruby calls, galloping over.

She seems more confident these days. A little more grown up. Stella would be proud. I know I am.

"Want to hear my new riddle?"

"Absolutely I do."

Ruby flaps her ears. She does that when she gets excited. "What has an eye but cannot see?"

"I am perplexed, Ruby. Pondering and puzzled."

"A hurricane!" she exclaims.

"Good one, Ruby. First-rate."

I look at Ivan. We smile at each other. We don't need to say a thing.

It's enough to listen to the palm trees rustle and watch the saw grass sway.

working on it

On the way home, we pass the shelter. It's been patched up pretty well, looks like. And they're back in business.

I hear the usual yelps and howls and hisses and meows, and like always, I feel lousy. I plop down on the sidewalk, and Julia stops walking.

"What's going on, Bob?" she asks.

I listen, like I always do, for her bark. *That* bark.

Nope. Nothing.

I wish Rowdy were here to distract me. But he's still learning how to walk on a tug-of-war string.

He's a pretty swell pup, even if he is a little feisty. I'm surprised how much I like having him around the house.

It's weird. I feel responsible for the little guy. Sorta like he's become my numero uno.

Julia bends down and strokes my head. I wag my tail a bit, slowly stand. I think of poor old Droolius stuck in that backyard, day and night. I think of Boss, roaming the streets. I think of my siblings, the dark night, the box, the highway.

I'm trying hard to find the forgiveness that seems to come so naturally to other dogs. Maybe that's what Boss was getting at. Maybe it's easier to forgive others once you've learned how to forgive yourself.

I'm working on it. It's like a bone. Sometimes you have to chew for a long time before you make any progress.

snickers, again

Once we're home, I head for the couch. I'm snoozing peacefully with Rowdy when a smell, a doozy of a smell, assaults my schnozz, which is finally back to working order.

It's *her*.

Snickers is back.

She's been gone for a while. After the hurricane, they had to do some repairs to Mack's house. Not sure where Snickers has been staying, but that's definitely her I smell, no doubt about it.

I dive under the couch, but not before Nutwit appears at the front window. "Oh, Bobbo!" he calls. "Someone's looking for you!"

"I'm not home," I yell.

"Yeah, I don't think she'll take no for an answer," says Nutwit.

"Shouldn't you be rebuilding your nest?"

"Naw. Watching you cower in fear is way more fun."

"What's the deal, Uncle Bob?" Rowdy asks.

"Be afraid, Rowdy," I say. "Be very afraid."

The door opens, and there's Julia with Snickers by her side.

"Well, hello there, Snickers," says Sara as she passes through the living room. "What are you doing here?"

"Mack and his wife just moved back in," Julia says. "They called this afternoon and said Snickers was dying for a walk."

I ease back a little farther under the couch. Can Snickers see me? Maybe not. But she can most definitely smell me.

For once I regret my pungent aroma.

Snickers darts across the living room straight to the couch, pulling Julia along for the ride.

"Snickers!" Julia exclaims. "Slow down, girl!" She kneels. "Bob, are you hiding under there?"

I move an inch, exposing my snout.

Snickers goes insane. She yanks free of her tug-of-war string. For a moment, she pauses to do a polite nose tap with Rowdy. Then she lets loose with zoomies and yips and howls of joy.

"Bob," Julia says, "come on out and say hi."

I pretend not to hear her. Which isn't a big stretch, since Snickers is barking like a maniac.

"Robert," says Julia.

Fine. I belly-crawl out until I'm exposed.

Snickers is ecstatic. She showers me with licks and nips and nudges and leaps. "Bob," she croons, "how I've missed you!"

I cover my head with my paws, but there's no escaping her adoration.

"There's a reason we survived, Bob," she says, her fuzzy tail in high gear. "The fates want our love to blossom."

"Is this your girlfriend, Uncle Bob?" Rowdy inquires.

"Girlfriend today," Snickers responds in a giddy voice. "But who knows what tomorrow may bring? Perhaps you should start calling me Aunt Snickers."

I am relieved beyond measure when Julia finally pulls Snickers, with great effort, out the door. I try to ignore Nutwit's teasing. I try to tolerate Rowdy's stifled laughter.

But when Minnie starts chanting "Bob and Snickers!" followed by Moo's "sitting in a tree!" I've had enough.

I head for my doggie door, ignoring the popcorning guinea pigs, and try to locate my dignity.

a visitor

This evening is like lots of other evenings.

The guinea pigs are squeaking. Nutwit is puttering in his tree. Julia and Sara and George are watching something about meerkats on the nature channel.

I've just settled in with Rowdy on the couch when George drops a cookie on the floor.

I leap into action.

"Robert," says Julia, "leave it."

Briefly, I consider my options. But not for long.

At least I share a piece with Rowdy.

"You are hopeless," Julia says. "But I love you anyway."

And that's when we hear the bark.

It's coming from the front porch.

"Hmm. That's weird," says George.

"I'll check it out." Julia runs to the door and pulls it open.

She hesitates.

She looks over at me, back at the porch, back at me.

"Bob?" she says. "I think it's for you."

And it is.

Author's Note

Dogs. Aren't they just the best?

If you answered "no," or even "yes" with a hint of ambivalence, um . . . what is wrong with you?

Sorry. Even if you're not on Team Canine, I'm sure you're a swell person. Maybe you're a cat fanatic, or a guinea pig fan. I get that. I love all kinds of creatures, right down to tarantulas and naked mole rats.

And I'll admit that some dogs are easier to love than others. My own mutt, Stan, is a case in point. Mercurial, needy, narcissistic, he's not exactly the poster dog for Man's Best Friend. Still and all, when Stan cuddles up just so (usually while I'm busy on my laptop), he somehow manages to pull off that mysterious canine magic trick: he makes me feel a little bit better about life.

Stan also serves as my muse, albeit sporadically. As a matter of fact, Bob, the narrator of this novel, was modeled on Stan, right down to the misanthropy, the gluttony, and the odor.

Bob originally appeared as a character in my novel *The One and Only Ivan*, inspired by the true story of a western lowland gorilla. The real Ivan spent twenty-seven years, alone and caged, in a shopping mall in Tacoma, Washington. Did he ever have a pal like Bob? I don't know. But there was a pet store at the mall where Ivan lived, and he had lots of visitors. It wasn't a stretch for me to imagine such a friendship evolving.

And so Bob was born. He had to be tiny, to fit in a hole in Ivan's cage. He had to be wily. He had to be a street dog: tough and blunt and no-nonsense. (You can imagine my delight when I learned that the inimitable Danny DeVito would be voicing Bob in the Disney *The One and Only Ivan* movie. Yep. That's Bob, all right.)

Bob's had a tough life. He's seen the darker side of humans. He doesn't really get the whole "man's best friend" thing. (His best friend, as it happens, is a gorilla.) He's carrying some pretty heavy baggage for such a little dog. And he faces down a lot in this story: tornadoes and owls, floods and wolves, terror and guilt and self-doubt.

But through it all, Bob never loses his tiny-mutt swagger. And he never stops listening to his good-dog heart.

Even if you're a devout cat person, I hope you enjoyed spending time with the guy.

Acknowledgments

Authors, like dogs, may seem like simple creatures. But beneath our shaggy exteriors, we require lots of support and TLC. *The One and Only Bob* would never have happened without the help of many lovely humans.

Endless gratitude goes to the fabulous folks at HarperCollins:

—Top Dogs: Suzanne Murphy, President & Publisher, and Jean McGinley, VP, Associate Publisher;

—Design: Amy Ryan and Sarah Pierson;

—Managing Editorial: Mark Rifkin, Renée Cafiero, and Valerie Shea;

—Assistant Editor: Sarah Homer;

—Marketing & Publicity: Nellie Kurtzman, Ann Dye, Jenn Corcoran, Audrey Diestelkamp, Vaishali Nayak, and Emily Zhu;

—Digital Marketing: Spencer Alben, Lindsay Jacobsen, Craig Kleila, Shae McDaniel, and Colleen O'Connell;

—School & Library: Patti Rosati, Mimi Rankin, and Katie Dutton;

—Audio: Caitlin Garing, Peter Bobinski, and Karen Radner;
—Everyone on the amazing HC sales team.

Special thanks and extra treats go to:

—Tara Weikum, my extraordinary editor, whose patience, good humor, flawless instincts, and unflagging support made writing this book a joy;
—Elena Giovinazzo, my brilliant and tireless agent at Pippin Properties;
—Patricia Castelao, for her gorgeous illustrations;
—Danny DeVito and Thea Sharrock, for their brilliant work on the audiobook;
—The original Ivan gang: Anne Hoppe, who helped me start the journey; Jodi Carrigan, Ivan's best friend and keeper; Donna Kouri and Colby Sharp, early and avid supporters of the book; and John Schumacher, whose love for children's literature knows no bounds;
—Gennifer Choldenko, Kathryn Otoshi, and Teri Sloat, my Rogue Colors support team;
—Mary Cate Stevenson and Noah Nofz at Two Cats Communications, who can do anything and do it brilliantly;

—Always and forever, my friends and family.

—And finally, thanks to the many readers of *The One and Only Ivan* who told me Bob needed a story of his own.

If you want to help gorillas, start here:

—The Dian Fossey Gorilla Fund International (www.gorillafund.org)

If you want to help elephants, start here:

—The Elephant Sanctuary in Tennessee (www.elephants.com)
—Sheldrick Wildlife Trust (www.sheldrickwildlifetrust.org)

If you want to help homeless pets, start here:

—Your local animal shelter—they always need a helping hand!

See where Ivan and Bob's story began
in this sneak peek at the Newbery Award–winning
and *New York Times* bestselling modern classic,
The One and Only Ivan!

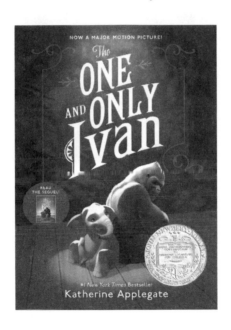

hello

I am Ivan. I am a gorilla.

It's not as easy as it looks.

names

People call me the Freeway Gorilla. The Ape at Exit 8. The One and Only Ivan, Mighty Silverback.

The names are mine, but they're not me. I am Ivan, just Ivan, only Ivan.

Humans waste words. They toss them like banana peels and leave them to rot.

Everyone knows the peels are the best part.

I suppose you think gorillas can't understand you. Of course, you also probably think we can't walk upright.

Try knuckle walking for an hour. You tell me: Which way is more fun?

patience

I've learned to understand human words over the years, but understanding human speech is not the same as understanding humans.

Humans speak too much. They chatter like chimps, crowding the world with their noise even when they have nothing to say.

It took me some time to recognize all those human sounds, to weave words into things. But I was patient.

Patient is a useful way to be when you're an ape.

Gorillas are as patient as stones. Humans, not so much.

how I look

I used to be a wild gorilla, and I still look the part.

I have a gorilla's shy gaze, a gorilla's sly smile. I wear a snowy saddle of fur, the uniform of a silverback. When the sun warms my back, I cast a gorilla's majestic shadow.

In my size humans see a test of themselves. They hear fighting words on the wind, when all I'm thinking is how the late-day sun reminds me of a ripe nectarine.

I'm mightier than any human, four hundred pounds of pure power. My body looks made for battle. My arms, outstretched, span taller than the tallest human.

My family tree spreads wide as well. I am a great ape, and you are a great ape, and so are chimpanzees and orangutans and bonobos, all of us distant and distrustful cousins.

I know this is troubling.

I too find it hard to believe there is a connection across time and space, linking me to a race of ill-mannered clowns.

Chimps. There's no excuse for them.

the exit 8 big top mall
and video arcade

I live in a human habitat called the Exit 8 Big Top Mall and Video Arcade. We are conveniently located off I-95, with shows at two, four, and seven, 365 days a year.

Mack says that when he answers the trilling telephone.

Mack works here at the mall. He is the boss.

I work here too. I am the gorilla.

At the Big Top Mall, a creaky-music carousel spins all day, and monkeys and parrots live amid the merchants. In the middle of the mall is a ring with benches where humans can sit on their rumps while they eat soft pretzels. The floor is covered with sawdust made of dead trees.

My domain is at one end of the ring. I live here because I am too much gorilla and not enough human.

Stella's domain is next to mine. Stella is an elephant. She and Bob, who is a dog, are my dearest friends.

At present, I do not have any gorilla friends.

My domain is made of thick glass and rusty metal and rough cement. Stella's domain is made of metal bars. The sun bears' domain is wood; the parrots' is wire mesh.

Three of my walls are glass. One of them is cracked, and a small piece, about the size of my hand, is missing from its bottom corner. I made the hole with a baseball bat Mack gave me for my sixth birthday. After that he took the bat away, but he let me keep the baseball that came with it.

A jungle scene is painted on one of my domain walls. It has a waterfall without water and flowers without scent and trees without roots. I didn't paint it, but I enjoy the way the shapes flow across my wall, even if it isn't much of a jungle.

I am lucky my domain has three windowed walls. I can see the whole mall and a bit of the world beyond: the frantic pinball machines, the pink billows of cotton candy, the vast and treeless parking lot.

Beyond the lot is a freeway where cars stampede without end. A giant sign at its edge beckons them to stop and rest like gazelles at a watering hole.

The sign is faded, the colors bleeding, but I know what it says. Mack read its words aloud one day: "COME TO THE EXIT 8 BIG TOP MALL AND VIDEO ARCADE, HOME OF THE ONE AND ONLY IVAN, MIGHTY SILVERBACK!"

Sadly, I cannot read, although I wish I could. Reading stories would make a fine way to fill my empty hours.

Once, however, I was able to enjoy a book left in my domain by one of my keepers.

It tasted like termite.

The freeway billboard has a drawing of Mack in his clown clothes and Stella on her hind legs and an angry animal with fierce eyes and unkempt hair.

That animal is supposed to be me, but the artist made a mistake. I am never angry.

Anger is precious. A silverback uses anger to maintain order and warn his troop of danger. When my father beat his chest, it was to say, *Beware, listen, I am in charge. I am angry to protect you, because that is what I was born to do.*

Here in my domain, there is no one to protect.

The Endling series by
KATHERINE APPLEGATE

The last of her kind.
The first to lead a revolt.

BOOK ONE   BOOK TWO   BOOK THREE

"Readers will fall in love with Byx and race with her through Nedarra, breathless and eager, thinking deeply all the way."

—*New York Times Book Review*

HARPER
An Imprint of HarperCollinsPublishers

harpercollinschildrens.com • endlingbooks.